THE WEDDING

AND OTHER STORIES BY CARA HOFFMAN

FACTORY SCHOOL 2006

THE WEDDING

AND OTHER STORIES BY CARA HOFFMAN

FACTORY SCHOOL 2006

Southpaw Culture

poetry to politics, pedagogy to planning

The Wedding and Other Stories

By Cara Hoffman

Factory School, 2006

ISBN 0-9711863-6-7

Front cover art by WormArt

Factory School is a learning and production collective engaged in action research, multiple-media arts, publishing, and community service.

For more information, please visit factoryschool.org.

WAKING

After the boys had taken their flushed faces and the lingering spirits of their breath down the steps and back to the car, we would stay up and watch the black-and-white films we had made, projected against the gray cement of the basement wall. It was as if the night were only just now starting, at one or two in the morning, and we were suddenly entirely ourselves. The projector hummed and clacked. The focus was primitive, and we dealt with it by moving the entire apparatus forward or backwards on its folding chair. The outside shots were often overexposed. Sometimes we watched these films projected against a mirror that hung near the laundry room door. Sometimes against a sheet. Sometimes I would read a novel out loud while we went through every reel, over and over. Once it was *The Sheltering Sky*. Once *The Trial*. And all the while fields flashed by, birds flew, fires burned, bicycles raced past, eyes blinked and mouths smiled. Image after image made of light.

This would end around nine or ten in the morning and then we would go outside, sleepless and energized, to walk beside the stone colored river. To walk along the trails. Sometimes we would shoot while we walked. Stills, super eight, Polaroids. *Polaroids*, she said, *said everything*. Their form alone. Their very being. The subject of the photograph itself was irrelevant. It was how it came to be. We filmed Polaroids as they developed. Pulling their plastic genius into the silent eloquent light.

And we never talked about the boys, once they were gone. We talked about the fastest way to get through school. You can, in tenth grade, graduate. You can. You do not even need perfect grades, just mediocre grades in upper level courses. But what would we do then? *What would we do then?* I asked. She just shook her head and smirked at me.

Stand over there, she said, pointing to a field of Queen Anne's Lace. *Go into the middle of it. Kneel. Stand. Stand with your head turned. Take off your coat. Put it back on. Do that thing with your arms where they look like they spin all the way around in front of you. Good.*

We didn't even think to show them the films. We didn't even film them. We didn't even give them books to read. We didn't even talk in the same tone of voice to them or when they were around. We said, *come over*. Or we said, *we'll meet you*. We said, *we'll be over later*. We didn't care what they did. We didn't care where they were when they weren't around. Disinterest sometimes made it necessary to terminate and replace. There was always another boy. Lying on the couch, sitting in the movie theater, or in the car. With the clothes they wore, with the seven day stubble, with stereo equipment and various talents, or interests gleaned from television. There was always another with his own "identity," immediate and plastic like a Polaroid. What exactly they provided during that time I can no longer remember.

I can remember the silent lips parting and the gray smoke drifting out. I can remember a shot, several seconds on the reel, of a girl skidding across the asphalt on her shin, grinning from the adrenaline before she took the skateboard up the halfpipe again. I can remember the shot of her lying in the grass laughing, her face wide and bright.

Run. And while you run, take off your clothes, till you are naked when you reach that tree, and then duck down in the grass to make it look like you were swallowed up by the earth. Good.

When the boys had taken their soft skin and their swollen mouths away we would walk outside in the dark. We would walk through the empty neighborhoods shining beneath the streetlights. Until we reached the abandoned downtown. The parking lots beneath the constellations. The tall buildings cutout against the black sky. The cool air. The expanse of concrete. This is how we walked then. In an enormous loop that lead back to the pools and gardens and fountains of the west side. And we swam behind our neighbor's houses, our quiet laughter drowned out by the sounds of crickets. We could smell the grass and the chlorine. Our breasts were weightless in the water. Like they weren't even there.

You can finish college at twenty. You can. You don't even need good grades. Just mediocre grades. You can finish at nineteen if you take twenty-four credits a semester. Then you're done. And you can go to graduate school then. You can finish grad school at twenty-two. You can have your Ph.D. by twenty-three. You *can*. You simply *can*. You can have at least three or four books written by then. You *can* be working for the Associated Press. You *can* study at a conservatory. You *can* sell guns. You *can* work in an orphanage. Smuggle spice out of the East.

We would make it home in those last crepuscular hours and hunch over the sink taking long draughts from the tap. We would sleep side by side on the floor in long white V-neck T-shirts. Our eyes moving back and forth beneath their lids. Our eyelashes resting against the tops of our cheekbones. Our mouths open, sucking in the night.

We slept this way until we saw how the boys were coming into finer focus. The boys pressed their bodies against our jeans in hayfields behind the monastery at night. And we saw more than their utility; we saw how they could be made beautiful. Inside the monastery basement, white candles burned for the dead, and outside in the fields the boys were ghostly images whose fascination lay in their unfolding and hardening form. But they were as yet interchangeable. Your fist closed around one just about the same as any another. And only one or two required further study, or became unique, sentimental items in their familiarity. Became desired. And once desired, ruined our sleep. Ruined our sleepless wandering.

It was like this in East Berlin, she'd said about the boys. She'd been in Berlin for three months studying art. The Wall was still standing then and she'd written our names on it.

She said there was the same brand of coffee on the shelf wherever you went. The same brand of aspirin. You couldn't get exactly the taste you wanted, but then you got used to whatever was there, and you liked it, no matter how crummy it was. No matter how weak it was. *They're not exactly Polaroids*, she corrected me. *They're like the coffee and the aspirin you buy in eastern Europe*, she said. *You needed it to stay awake, or not feel pain, and if it wasn't working you just had more. They're like that.*

Don't move, she said, in the grass outside the monastery. *Don't move at all. It looks like you're a statue. It looks like you're a monument. You're a statue of the virgin skater. The great fallen tomboy.* And she laughed. *We'll show them this film*, she said. *We'll have the coffee and the aspirin over for movies. I should shoot you from the back*, she said, *as I walk away. I should shoot this on nitrate film, so it will burn up if we leave it in the sun!*

They sat and watched the films with us in the dark basement; the films of the Polaroids developing, and the overexposed films, and the statue, and the girl swallowed by the earth. Their faces were luminescent. Reflections of images passed over them like the shadows of clouds moving over the land.

After the reels were done and our eyes had adjusted, we didn't turn on the lights. We didn't ask them what they thought. We didn't offer them a drink. We didn't kiss. Or feel them. We just sat there in the dark.

That was a good night, she'd said about it. *In retrospect, it seems you should have slept with one of them. It seems we should have done something other than rewind the films. Maybe we should bring them on a walk next time. Maybe we should bring them swimming.*

And then we slept on the couch in our clothes. Our long hair braided together on one side: blond, black, blond, black, blond. The tiny pale hairs on our cheeks nearly touching. And just before unconsciousness I could hear how her breathing was like her voice, how her throat held her voice and was full of sound and meaning, even as she quietly exhaled.

You can leave and never come back. You can stop speaking entirely and carry a little chalkboard with you on a rope around your neck. She laughed. *Because you can see how everything here is something other than what it is, can't you? Every blade of grass, every word, every inflection. Certainly you can see that now*, she said. *You can see that silence is the whiteness of the sheet in the basement. And that we are waiting.*

Waiting and waiting, we said in unison and I nodded.

She said, *right now it's as bright as heaven. It's as clear as night.* The music of her voice carried as she spoke, like a little song, and I stopped walking to light my cigarette.

This whole beautiful world, she said, tears running down her face at last, as she grabbed the collar of my shirt, *is a lie.*

THE MOUSE'S SISTER

They found the mouse's sister in the basement. She had lost a fingernail, and the skin on the finger from which it was missing was blue. Her fur was patchy and oily looking. Her face revealed that she was trying to remember something. Eyes lifted and faraway. She was sitting on her hind legs, one hand tucked into her fur and the damaged one extended, the bruised finger pointing of its own volition towards the hurricane door.

The mouse himself was gone and said to be living in a couch in the southern part of the city, working on a scientific project that would one day turn snow into food.

When they found her, they brought her back behind the base-boards and said she'd missed two days of school. It was bad luck to ask why, so no one did. Her fur was hot, and her hands and feet were hot and her tongue was dry. Her expression had settled into a squint and it looked like she was about to remember, but she didn't.

She ate the orange peels that had been brought to her. They thought she had been given messages for a new project because she was hungry and hunger is where messages and prayers originated. They thought she had become religious because she ate now in answer to prayers.

"No, I didn't pray for oranges," she told them when she had finished, and again she had that look, like she was trying to remember. She rubbed her little finger against her gum.

"Your brother is still working on the snow project," they told her. Whenever they said the word "snow" they whispered it. And she thought, listening to them, I will never whisper the word snow again. She knew this was true but had no idea why it was so. *I will never whisper snow*, she thought. *I will never whisper dog. I will never whisper trap. I will never whisper cat. I will never whisper snake.* And it seemed like the sentences were steps, were smells, and that she was walking up a little path that cooled her skin and wet her tongue as she got closer to the end of it. She squinted harder to see what was at the end of it.

"Were you given a message?" they asked. And one of her sisters patted down her fur.

"No," she said.

"You can reveal it." And again they whispered when they said the word reveal. *I will never whisper reveal*, the mouse's sister thought. *I will never whisper snake. I will never whisper cold. I will never whisper bird.*

"Did you find some poison?" They asked. *I will never whisper poi-*

son, she thought, her skin felt cooler and she squinted off into the distance, getting closer to the end of the little path in her mind with every sentence.

They left her behind the baseboard. They said tomorrow there was school. Her face was still set in brooding. Whatever it was she had forgotten, she thought, she couldn't have known it by heart. She would keep chewing on it. It was like she was building the exit, she thought. First it's a wall then it's a space. You just keep chewing.

She sat on her hind legs, leaning against a pile of lint and cardboard tucked between the wall and an electrical cable. Her blue finger pointed down the long corridor, at little blades of light radiating in from around the nails that shot through her room. They were like rays of a black-centered sun.

*

The schoolmaster didn't ask where she had been because it was bad luck.

He said, "Here, you've missed a lot. This is what the air smells like beneath the tree in which the owl sits. This is the number of stitches to cast on when you are knitting a cap. A great project is now underway that will make us free. Your brother is involved. He is risking himself. He is making sacrifices in his standard of living."

When she left the classroom, the corridors smelled like something decomposing. All around her she could smell it and she had to run to the toilet and vomit.

Her sisters were combing their hair in front of a strip of aluminum foil that hung above three square white sinks.

"Are you okay?" they asked.

"Yes," the mouse's sister said. "It's that smell in the hallway. Can't you smell it?"

They turned their heads towards the door and raised their noses. "We smell orange peel and stomach bile."

"Can't you smell that other smell?"

"No," they said. Their shoe laces had pictures of cherries and strawberries on them.

The mouse's sister stood beside them and looked at the warped reflection of her squinting face. She raised her hands to her whiskers and saw the crooked blue finger.

"It's time to go," her sisters said. "It's time to go to class." They put their combs in their school bags and left through the round door.

In the next class they watched a play. The mouse's sister dozed and felt hot. The play was about the preparations made by those who were called for the snow project. Six mice wearing caps walked across a stage and three mice threw wood shavings into the air. One mouse pretended to be dead and in the end they ate the wood shavings. *Sacrifice for Freedom from Scarcity and Cold* was the name of the play. In her mind she shouted *scarcity* and then *cold*. And then *owl*. And the path opened before her in her fevered dreamy state, and her face reflected the stillness of one who is about to hear something.

When had any of them felt cold? Or known scarcity? In her mind, the path raised up and she could not see beyond the crest of a little hill, but she thought she could almost make out the whiskers on berries she was certain would be growing there. Her fur felt wet. She felt like she was living inside a stove. And she could faintly detect that smell again.

Snow, she thought, white and thick like a layer of fat, came floating down to stiffen the world. It always came. There was nothing to fear in it. They lived inside the cut flesh of trees, gone dry and dead. And stones put all together. All those things smelled different from the world, smelled like the idea for the snow project, smelled like they had come from hunger. And had that paltry tattered quality, of visions that are manufactured, that are run through the machinery of their bodies to make them alert and whisper. Snow did not smell like that. Snow was not an idea. It was not different from the world.

All the things that came from nowhere were indisputably true. All the things like snow and air and rain. She did not want these things changed. She did not want hunger to bring messages. She did not think changing a thing that came from nowhere could feed anyone. She wanted to eat insects. She wanted to eat rye. The mouse's sister wanted snow and snakes and dogs and cold. Because, in the basement, she had seen the things that should really be spoken about in a whisper.

*

She had felt at once how the air down inside the walled-off earth was different from the rest of the priorate. There was a closeness to things, and she felt she could walk slowly or sit up and listen for a long time. She felt how the basement was the seed of the priorate, and all the other nests and the school owed something to it.

She watched something move over by the stone wall and then made her way rapidly to it, stopping again to sit and observe it from behind a metal pole. There beneath a squat square of light stood another mouse. He had captured a bee and had tied it on a leash. He would let the bee fly up towards the square and then jerk it back down so that it hit the floor. The thing was missing legs and its voice was hoarse from trying to reason with the mouse. It was thirsty.

This bee was the sole survivor of a group of brothers who strayed once they had entered the priorate by mistake. They had heard something in the basement, but it had turned out to be jars of jam. You cannot dance directions to the sound of jars of jam, and so they tried to leave. The desiccated carcasses of the bee's brothers lay half eaten near the wall beneath the squat square of light.

"It's not right for you to eat them," she heard the bee tell the mouse. He sighed and hovered just before the mouse's face, waving his remaining legs in a frantic involuntary motion. "*I* am to eat my brothers. My *brothers* are to eat my brothers. All of our children are to eat us. Not you." His tone revealed that this was a speech he had been making over and over for some time. And it seemed to the mouse's sister that he had lost his mind.

The mouse jerked the bee again and he bounced roughly off the floor. "Our home is of our body, our food is of our body," the bee said, his voice cracking with emotion. "We build from nothing. Each of us is one and all of us is one." The mouse laughed at him; his eyes were excited and bulged forward from their red rims like black mirrors. And the yellow reflection of the trapped bee moved over their surface like little flames flickering up from deep inside him. "You eat garbage and you are food," the bee went on. "You are illness. Let us go. You are illness." The bee waved his stinger about. He was thirsty. He was the sole living bee, and the mouse's sister was certain now that in his grief he had lost his mind; that being leashed by this mouse had destroyed him. She wondered why the mouse didn't simply eat him or let him go. Why he didn't finish the other bees, which looked very appetizing to her.

She moved quickly into his field of vision and stood silent. The bee became more agitated. The mouse spoke to her.

"What are you doing down in the walled-off earth?" he asked her pleasantly, but his eyes still bulged and flickered with the yellow reflection.

"I go where I like," she told him. The bee was silent now, terrified.

"Your brother is working on the snow project, isn't he?"

"Yes," she said.

"I've been to that couch," he told her boastfully. "I recognize your look. You look like your brother and a number of those who were called. They were from the same birth, but your brother has your same exact face."

She nodded.

"Let me go," the bee said.

"In the couch," the mouse went on, "they are living on top of one another. They are breeding with mice that lived there before they arrived. Those mice whisper every word they say, not just words like *fire*. I worked on that project. I know what that project is."

The mouse's sister nodded. He's insane as well, she thought, and eyed the bee corpses.

"They are eating all their young as they are born. And they have learned a new language which consists entirely of shouts and in which there is no word for snow."

"*Kill him*," the bee shouted suddenly to the mouse's sister. And the mouse reeled the bee in and clutched him by his wings, holding him at arms length out in front of her. His black eyes now made up entirely of the yellow reflection. "I've been chained to him most of my life," the bee said, waving his remaining legs. "All this, for what turned out to be jam."

"Are your food and your home really made from your body?" the mouse's sister asked the captive bee, "are all of you really one?" He shook himself in exasperation.

The bee jerked himself to and fro in the mouse's hands and waved his stinger about. "Kill him," he said again. The yellow in the mouse's eyes grew and receded, and then all at once he thrust the bee forward.

The mouse's sister put her hand out to cover herself. The stinger shot through her palm just below the right index finger and nailed her hand to the opposite shoulder. She stood like that looking at the other mouse with her arm across her body until he yanked the bee away. The inside of its body clung to the stinger and hung down the front of her. And the silent shell of the sole bee was tossed to the floor still wearing its leash.

The yellow vanished from the mouse's eyes, and they turned black and flat and empty like holes. "It is they that are illness," the mouse said to her. "It is they that are food," he said. His voice was like his eyes. And then he moved quickly away from her.

The bee venom put the mouse's sister to sleep. When she awoke she pulled the stinger out. She ate the bodies of the bee and his brothers. Then she stood for two days. Her hand swelled and her fingernail dropped off. And it was then she first smelled, but only faintly, that odor of something decomposing.

ʌ

She smelled it now at her desk. The odor was all around and she didn't know why her sisters couldn't smell it. Her hand had turned a blackish green and the finger burned. It had its own heart. It itched terribly and was hot. She pressed it against the cool desktop, which offered only seconds of relief before making it worse. Then she held the finger out in the air and this made it feel better for a moment before it itched so badly she had to scrape her teeth against it. And all the while the smell grew, nauseating her.

The school master said, "What did we learn from the play?"

"We learned about sacrifice," her sisters said.

"And what else?" he asked, writing the word on the chalkboard.

"Food?"

"Yes," he wrote this as well. "And what else?"

"There is a great threat of scarcity," they said. When he wrote this he abbreviated the words with a lowercase "t" and a lower case "s."

"They don't know the word for s-n-o-w anymore," the mouse's

sister said.

"No, but it does have to do with that word."

"They are turning snow into food," one of the brightest sisters said.

"Right." He wrote "food" on the chalkboard. "Very good."

"And they are breeding and then eating the young," the mouse's sister said, still scraping her finger against her teeth, "because they have no room and have wed slave mice who only know how to speak in whispers."

"No," said the schoolmaster, "but they *are* making sacrifices in their standard of living."

"I don't think my brother would want to sire slave mice. I think he'd eat them if he did."

It was bad luck to respond, so they spoke about paper bags, paper plates and cake. She tried to walk up the little path in her mind again to soothe her bruised finger and cool her body. But this time she couldn't see it.

After school her sisters asked her, "Why did you give those answers?"

"Can't you smell that?" she asked them.

"No," they said.

She bit at the finger and a cold wire shot from where her teeth touched right through her. She shuddered, then bit some more. It was all right. It hurt enough and it was starting to hurt in other places. If it was gone it would not be sore. It was like building an exit.

Back behind the baseboard she leaned against the pile of lint and chewed at her blue hand until it was gone. Then she slept. When she awoke, the smell was there behind the baseboards. She watched the blades of light shining through the nail holes and felt no pain from her handless wrist. The white bone shone from inside the clean cut.

Without the pain, the odor was more tolerable. Now she extended the remaining hand and tucked the stump into her fur.

At school her sisters asked her, "Why have you eaten your hand?"

"It was painful, now it's gone."

"How will you get on in your studies without it?"

"Can you smell that?" she asked them.

They said, "No, we can't. We can't."

The mouse's sister nodded. She went to the bathroom with them and they combed their hair. She watched them moving their hands, scraping the comb against their heads over and over. As if they were extracting something from inside themselves. Maybe this combing is how they get information. Maybe this combing brings the correct answers to scholarly questions, the mouse's sister thought.

She pulled a tissue out of her pocket and blew her nose. At this her sisters stopped their combing and raised their noses in her direction. They were quiet for one second. "We can smell it now," they said looking at her. After a few moments they asked, "What are you trying to remember?"

She opened the tissue and peered inside It was the color of black-berries and the consistency of molasses.

"This is the source of the smell," she said.

"Yes. That is definitely the source of the smell," they said. And this time they whispered the word smell. "It's time to go to," they said. "It's time to go to class."

It was bad luck to speak about her missing hand, so the school-master didn't. He said, "Today we are listening to a choir. They are singing about the freedom we will soon have."

The choir was made up of slightly older mice all wearing red blazers. Every one of them could make their face look as if they had just found a sack of oats. I wonder if we'll get the oats after their song, the mouse's sister thought. The choirmaster held out a white wand that gave the choir information. The wand was still and mute and beautiful, slender like the bones in her arm, strong and pliable. It poked the air and they began to sing. And she saw that their eyes bulged like the eyes of the mouse in the basement had, and that the wand moved inside their eyes like the reflection of the bee. The wand chopped and poked, duplicated in the sets of eyes. Just like the bee, it wasn't itself once it had gotten trapped in there. In the eyes of the choir, the wand was something thin and sharp but no longer straight. In the eyes of the choir, it was a little white whip. The mouse's sister thought maybe they had lost their minds like the mouse in the basement. Some of them looked as if they could be from the same birth as that mouse.

She still could smell the odor of decay, but now that she knew it was coming from inside her nose, she felt she might be able to get rid of it. She dozed as they sang, waking for the crescendos, and in parts where they had to clap their hands or stomp their feet.

One song was all about a paper bag under a sink, and another was about feeding barley to the young. Another song was about not eating soap. Then there was a solo about some very soft insulation. The ending number was about the snow project, and they marched in place as they sang it.

When they finished, the choirmaster put the wand away and their eyes sank deeper into their heads and shone nothing. Everyone clapped. The mouse's sister did not have to clap.

"What did we learn from the songs?" the schoolmaster asked later.

"Insulation is good for nests," her sisters said.

"Right, and what else?"

"We always need more food," they said. "For the young," they added after a moment.

"Right."

"The best place to find a paper bag is under a sink."

"Very good," the schoolmaster nodded.

"Bee's make both their homes and their food from nothing."

"No," the schoolmaster said. "But there is the letter B in something we learned."

"We have to *be* quiet," her sisters said.

"Yes, Yes. Very good. What else?"

"We are food," the mouse's sister said. "And we live by stealing. And the young taste very good."

It was bad luck to respond. So the schoolmaster ended the lesson by telling them that there were many more words that should be spoken in whispers. And that some whispered words didn't really exist at all. Then he let them leave early.

The mouse's sister blew more of the sticky substance out of her nose as she made her way back home. It smelled like a grave. Her face revealed that she was trying to remember something.

It was a mistake to have blown her nose because now it was running freely. Someone is building an exit, she said to herself. *Cold*, she shouted in her mind, leaning back on the electrical cable. *Scarcity*, *reveal*, *snow*, *trap*, *cat*. And she could no longer smell the grave smell coming from inside her. *Cake*, she whispered aloud. *Food*, she whispered, *paper bag*, *paper plate*, *grain*. And she could see again the little road. The crest of the hill sunk with each step she took, so that she could see over the top and beyond. And there, just as she had suspected, were berries, and the road smelled like the inside of her head, like mud, but with nothing decomposing in it. The berries were round. Each one made up of thousands of little round sacs, and they had little whiskers growing in the cracks between the sacs that made up the roundness. Each of them is one and all of them is one, she said to herself. And she felt a great thirst. Her eyes shone with what her whispers had revealed to her. They reflected only what was inside her head, and nothing else. Not a sole slave bee nor a white whip. Her eyes were like flat black mirrors, raised so that they could never catch the look of one who passed by them; one who passed, glancing for their own reflection in them. Her eyes were raised and calm and still like water. And she could see the road and the hedge-row of berries, but they did not shine greedily on the surface of her face. *Dog*, she shouted. *Bird, snake*, she shouted. And she followed the little path backwards until it reached through the black centered suns in the baseboard, and ended at a pool of something dark and sticky she had been standing in. The little path came from nowhere right to her feet.

She left the ambry and made her way out to the rest of the priori-ate which was made from the silent insides of trees. She could still see the path. She moved quickly and her sharp white toes struck rapidly and barely audible against the mute boards. She crossed through the center of the priorate and saw her sister's faces poking out of their separate nests, their eyes shining.

"Your brother has not returned from the project yet," they called to her. "We will learn the songs to sing to him and to the other con-scripts when we go to school."

She said nothing in reply. She looked as if she were trying to re-member something.

She stopped when she reached a cupboard and then turned a cor-ner, and followed the path along the side of the baseboard until she reached a long strip of light as wide as her body and as tall as the priorate. The long crack of light shone in her sister's eyes, curving over the surface of them.

"You won't learn a thing inside that little sliver of light," they called to her as she slipped through it.

Something invisible ran itself over her body, like all the hands of her sisters pressing her fur down at once. Like an invisible comb that could comb everywhere at once. She knew her sisters would like it better than their own small combs. It pressed against her face and made itself minute and entered her nostrils. She opened her mouth and swallowed some of it. She saw her fur moving under the power of this invisible comb.

Dog, she shouted aloud at the top of her lungs, *Dog, poison, owl, fire*. She pointed the stub of her right hand in the direction of the little hill. She could smell the grain all around her, young grain inside a smell of water. She could smell the earth.

She could hear the voices of insects and the hum of the insides of trees as the dark syrup poured from her nose. It burst forth from her sinuses. She opened her mouth and it poured from her as if all that was inside of her was black honey. As if inside of her was another mouse made up entirely of a liquid grave. Obviously that mouse couldn't live inside the crack of light. She would leave it there on the doorstep of the priorate.

Poison, Trap, Cat! she shouted. The last of the other mouse trickled out of her nose and stuck to her fur. She began to run. She reached a hollow between the earth and the stump of an old maple that was murmuring the last of an historical essay on crows. The mouse's sister put her ear against his crumbling side, and saw hanging beside her, the gray blue thorns, and the hundreds of red sacs that made up the roundness of a berry.

Food, she whispered, raising herself up so that her whiskers brushed the whiskers of the berry. *Food*, she whispered, and raised her mouth to fill herself with its blood.

THE PARAGRAPHER

Flynn is trying to hold it together with the details. The names, the dates, and times. The locations and the descriptions of these locations will impose a sense of reality on what has otherwise become a barrage of random, terrifying and unverifiable images. Right now, for Flynn, the center does not hold, and eight hundred words and a by-line will not bring things together in a neat package.

From a distance she can see that the crew has already gathered. Yellow tape is strung from tree to tree and there are men with radios at the periphery. The snowflakes are large and coming down fast. They settle thickly on the black branches of trees surrounding the site, drawing all sound nearer, up into itself. Her boots do not crack through the surface rigor mortis of yesterday's snowfall; one hundred pounds, she is held aloft on it, even at her hasty gait. Today's snow packs itself into the black treads of her soles. The hollows of her shallow footprints fill in behind her.

Lights have been set up. The pile of dirt beside the dig is already covered in white. White everywhere. They are about to strike something that will give in a wholly different way, the men with shovels and men with radios, the ambulance driver, channels seven and fifteen, suited and lipsticked, and in the dimming light, silent and slight, among the depredators and fingersmiths, Flynn.

*

Flynn taps the replay on the transcriber, and the voice of White's best friend slides through the headphones and into her ears. This has been going on for close to a year. Her foot hits the transcriber, and then voices push into her head. Her fingers strike the lettered keys concordant with the sounds, and her eyes stare at the screen, reflecting each word as it forms, on a glassy sheen covering a web of broken blood vessels.

In this way she closes a circuit around Wendy White's life. The who, what, when, where of it. The accumulation of details. The testimonies and vacuities that lead where they always do. Flynn has listened to the sentences so many times she can account for every pause, every raised intonation, every "uh" or cough that the tape repeats.

"the cops. And then we filed all the paperwork, like, on that Tuesday and it was fuckin'—can I say—"

"filed all the paperwork, like, on that Tuesday and it was fuckin'—can I say—"

"ke, on that Tuesday and it was fuckin'—can I say fu—"

"and it was fuckin'—can I say fuck? Ah, you won't put that in right? Anyway, just a sec… okay, so by Friday we were like—"

"put that in right? Anyway, just a sec… okay, so by Friday we were like—"

y Friday we were like, man! Something fucked up has happened, y'know? And we were like, aren't they gonna look for her? 'Cause—"

"ked up has happened, y'know? And we were like, aren't they gonna look for her? cause—"

"onna look for her? 'Cause sh—"

*

Flynn is in the back seat looking out. She can see the girl's breath dissipating as it rises towards the street light to the right of the driveway on Lisbon Avenue. She watches the white vapor for a while before she realizes what it is, realizes that it's coming out of Sarah's mouth, rising from her lungs, up through her body, and then ascending to mingle with the light and factory blowover. Sarah is standing beside the '87 Chevy, peering into the glass that has gone reflective in the dark.

Sarah's trying to see inside but has to get closer before she can. Her breath steams up the back seat window and she rubs it clear with a thinsulate mitten. She presses her face close to the glass again and curves her hands over her forehead and at the sides of her temples to block out the glare. Seeing Flynn, she raises her eyebrows and smiles involuntarily, but getting a closer look makes her turn and crunch back up the driveway.

Flynn hears the faint stridulation of the storm door and then Sarah's bundled shoulder hitting the wood of the interior door to press it open. Then the hollow stamping of boots on the carpet of the landing. And the clear audio from the TV, a chorus of sylphadine voices singing about razor blades and the smoothness of a man's face. The voices sound happy and Flynn knows that kind of resonation is achieved either by smiling while singing, or holding the skin on the side of your face back to widen your lips and create a flatter, upwardly arced, resonating cavity within your skull.

"She's still crying, Dad," the girl calls out from the doorway where she stands in her socks. One of them is inside out and she pulls at the ridged end of its seam, leaning against the door frame, back from her brief trek down the driveway.

"Okay now. Leave. Her. Alone. Sarah, I *told* you….."

Then the snug seal of the door, a muffled squeak and quiet.

The snow swirls in the light of the lamp and four or five boys pass, walking in the middle of the road where it's plowed. Flynn watches them as if she's at the drive-in, as if their forms are projected on rain-damaged rippling fabric one hundred yards away.

She doesn't know how many hours she's been sitting in the car, because it's been dark all the while. The light pollution has done little to obscure the stars, and she has watched them slip up beyond the tops of the windows. She lies now, comfortable in the Chevy's massive back seat, weeping. The space is bigger than the couch in her apartment. Her face is sticky, is alternately warm and freezing. Her red hair is plastered to her cheeks. It is wet inside her ears. She is still holding her pencil.

She is happy that no one has shown up for a while now to look at her, that no one has asked if she'd like to go somewhere or come in and warm up. It's actually not bad with the blanket and her body heat in the confined space. She breathes easily and continues to sob, resigned to it. It's second nature now. She can laugh while doing it, carry on a conversation… anything. Yesterday this wouldn't have seemed possible. Yesterday, before she got her big break.

*

"Flynn. Turns out it *is* that site by the reservation. Good work, girl!"

Flynn is standing before she realizes it, her chair rolling back towards the curved industrial glass of the water cooler.

"C'mon," Joe claps his hands. "If it bleeds, it leads." She can smell his breath from the doorframe where he leans. It smells like coffee that's been left in the pot all night and reheated. "C'mon," he says again, but he doesn't have to, because she already has her boots back on. "C'mon. Lets *move* it."

Flynn is leaving the office with her coat in her hand, her narrow reporter's notebook, she looks for her pen for a moment and then realizes she is already holding one in her mouth, and another one in her left hand. There's a pencil impaling a knot of hair at the base of her neck.

"And if you get a chance, pick up a carton of Marlboros, 'cause they're tax free on the res. You people are driving me fucking loony, nickel and diming me to pay for smokes. This is the last time." He hands her a twenty. "Cigarettes are not office supplies."

He looks at her full in the face for a moment. Then nods with the weight of where she's headed, claps his hands. "Alright kiddo. Take the stairs, if you wait for the elevator you'll get caught in rush hour, and it'll be dark when you get there."

He says "when you get there" to a closed door, because she's down one flight and swinging herself around at the end of the banister. The fear of getting there at all makes her sprint nervously. When she reaches the sidewalk, she runs through the hard little flecks of snow that blow across Franklin Street, down from the buildings and up from the gray plowed roads. They hit her face with the weight of iron filings and she is certain that more than two are alike, that they are somehow *all* the same, these cold white ghosts of fingerprints raining down on her cheeks.

"r her? 'Cause she's been gone for a week and all her stuff is—"
"for a week and all her stuff is at the apartment and her b—"
"artment and her boyfriend is freaking out, like ready to fu—"

*

Now Flynn is turning to dust in the back of an '87 Chevy on Lisbon Avenue. Flynn is traveling back in time, back eight months, and then another eight, and then another, back beyond the missing Wendy White. Back beyond Wendy White's famous disappearance and her still only-imagined murder. Back before Flynn had consciously built her career on the hair and sperm in the couch and the blood in the car. Flynn is sinking beneath the rim of the world of Wendy White. She drifts down through the snow, and curls mutely on the frozen asphalt, so that she may bloom when things have melted, so that she may re-emerge when it's warm, younger still, and in another driveway, as little Flynn, fifteen years old.

There in the car now she can feel the vibration and roll of the skateboard beneath her feet. She tilts her body as she heads up the half pipe, shoots off the lip and twists to face the other way. She places her hand on the rim of the curve, willing all the strength of her arm to keep her up, her hair hangs down, her bent knees support the board, the wheels coast on their ball bearings. Her feet are anxious to make that connection, and come sliding down the pipe in the opposite direction. And then to do it again, and again, and again. This was the only thing besides reporting that Flynn had ever felt her body and mind were made for.

While she skated, that song would come streaming out of the upstairs window at the back of the house, that serious question that she always thought was a joke… "Why can't I get just one kiss? Why can't I get just one kiss? Maybe some things I wouldn't miss but I've waited my whole life for just one…."

And then the short, steep ramp and upward curve of the half pipe again, a baby rocking to sleep in a cradle of concrete construction refuse. If only she could balance now on one arm and guide the resupine board back on its course.

If only she could get out and write something simple on the service workers' strike, on the curfew or on toxic factory blowover, a piece on some nonspecific egalitarian brutality. Flynn loves those assignments. Flynn would kill for some five o'clock shadow but instead she wears her long red hair in a knot haphazardly impaled with a blue proofing pencil. She wears gold wire-rimmed glasses, faded jeans, and a frayed white oxford shirt with a man's black cardigan over top.

She would do this job for nothing. She would pay somebody else to be able to look and act as she does. She gathers information like the latch-key girl she was, tasting the apple core forgotten beneath the couch, reading every book, riffling through the desks and under-wear drawers. She was in her element there, as she had been in the half pipe. Alone and moving through it, in love with the idea and the motion, and each properly executed turn.

She loves that politicians lie. She loves her press pass with the city seal and signatures on the back. She loves that cops really do leave blood and glass in the street and that other cops let her get right up close to it. She loves that her profession is largely based in fact check-ing, and forcing others to be accountable. She loves that the paper's archive is called a "morgue," and that the evening of deadline is called "putting the paper to bed." She loves turning the phrase that will lay everything bare, make all the connections. She gets paid to watch for subtleties, gets paid to be untrusted. To be ethical. To have hope. To see things, and let them feed upon her, and somehow turn it around. Because somewhere, she knows, there's a collective *good*. If people *understand*, if they get information, they will do the *right* thing.

And in some way, even a murder could be rectified, if people just knew more. Or if the prose were good enough, or if Flynn herself became harder, and colder, became a tomb around her own heart. A walking tomb that could drag everything to light, that could, with language, with verification, slip meaning into the public discourse. Like slipping a pill into a dog's mouth by hiding it in a piece of meat. This is why Flynn works like she does. This is how she earned her nickname. This is why she's running in the vespertine, in midwinter, to get to a gravesite at a location she had predicted, before all the good light is gone.

But it turns out that this uncovering speaks for itself. There's nothing more to be said. The makeover in language and narrative that she would apply to brutality and banality is itself more grotesque than the actual events. And the point at which Flynn balances, the arc where she hangs, tucked upside down and supported on one thin arm, this combination of hope, skill, time and luck, no longer adds up. No longer exists. This combination, she realizes sitting in the car on Lisbon Avenue, is extinct.

*

All four of the boys are looking into the car now, hands cupped around faces and sealed tight to the window. The older boy's eyes peer in and then shift to the sides to look at one another. Sarah is chewing a wad of gum, and she absently blows a bubble that touches the glass. Her brother turns, tries to pop it, but it's frozen, and his finger cracks it like it's ice. They laugh and she pulls it out of her mouth to look at it. She puts it back in and chews harder, seeming to use all the muscles in her jaw, neck and shoulders to soften it up. They all look at Flynn, hopefully, to see if she thinks it's funny. This starts her sobbing again.

"Flynn," Gabe says, rapping one knuckle on the glass before her face. His voice is muffled. "It's eleven o'clock."

"Yeah," she says wiping her face. "I figured it was late."

"Why don't you get out of the fucking *car* then?" Jesse asks her.

"Ah, I'm planning on staying in the car." She is crying openly now. The conversation is no problem. Weeping has become like breathing.

She hears the storm door swing shut and more crunching down

the driveway.

She can see the outline of Joe approaching in his Carhartt and fake-fur hat.

They turn their pale rosy faces to him, and she watches their breath rise white about their father.

"Would you guys get the hell away from the car like I asked you?" He opens the back door and tosses in another rolled-up wool blanket and a bag of tortilla chips.

"Thanks," Flynn tells him, still weeping.

"I *mean* it," he says to his kids. They range in height from four feet to five foot eight, steadily gaining on him every day. They all have dark brown eyes and the same round pale faces. It's as if he created the same child over and over of different ages. And they all, even the girl, resemble him, but for his blue eyes.

They turn and trudge defiantly back up the drive way, hunching their shoulders as if they are actually *dis*obeying him.

*

After the bars close, loud college boys, and quiet, slow walking home boys make their way back through the neighborhood in groups or solitary, coming either from Anacones or Micky Rat's. They cross back into their own neighborhoods without a word to one another. A similar ritual was being carried out now on the Westside too, she thought. Only the parties crossing were slightly different. Drunken criminology majors, and art therapy majors with lower SAT scores and less family income, were passing by bandanna-wearing esses who wore less leather, and, statistically, carried more firearms. It was that demographic she had watched pass by, on the evening she took her tape recorder down to the scene. The evening she had a walk-through with Officer Tallon.

*

"All I can tell you right now is that they are being held for questioning because of—"

"I can tell you right now is that they are being held for questioning because of a report from neighbors that a loud—"

"ing because of a report from neighbors that a loud and disturbing noise was emanating from the apart—"

"Noise was emanating from the apartment. This turned out to be an electric sander. Officers arrived at apr—"

*

In the summer she used to take Joe's kids to a beach on Lake Erie across the Peace Bridge. It was a crowded strip of public waterfront at the end of a narrow winding road near the remains of an abandoned amusement park. The great skeleton of a rollercoaster jutted up, black and ridged against the gray waterfront sky. And it was against this backdrop that she swam with her editor's dark-haired children, in water that she knew was contaminated with PCBs and heavy metals. But was warm and got deep gradually, and the Kullman kids ran in the waves and built things in the sand. Once a week in summer, to play by the great old remains of the park, to absorb the detritus that is your city's legacy, to see the seraphic order of its industrial skyline, while coming home over the Peace Bridge, is better than watching TV or trying to dig a moat around your house on the Northside.

On the way home in the car, the whole ungrateful brood of them would sing *Smells Like Teen Spirit*, *This Land is Your Land*, *Fifteen Miles on the Erie Canal*, and always, *Dirty Old Town*. It was something to hear, especially *Dirty Old Town*. When she pulled her noisy Volkswagen into the drive, they would pile out and there would be sand and dirt all over the floor and the seats would be wet with their cheek marks.

*

"*Officers arrived at approximately three ten in the morning to check on th*"

"*ten in the morning to check on the disturbance report and found… here you can see where it…yeah… Ro*"

"*bance report and found…here you can see where it…yeah… Roberts and Bectel sanding Bectel's living room floor.*"

*

It's still dark when Joe's wife, Marie, wakes her up. She opens the door and sits in the back next to her. Flynn has been crying in her sleep and it has created a constant, almost comforting state. It has erased the transition from sleeping to waking with its regularity.

"Boy. It's *cold* in here," Marie tells her. She reaches into the bag of chips and eats one, talking with her mouth full. "I guess you had a bad day, huh? We were worried about you."

Flynn's eyes are nearly swollen shut. Marie eats another chip. "Well, I just wanted to see if you were warm enough. You know it's about three now?"

"Oh, is it?"

"Yeah," Marie says gently. "You know, if you wanted to, you could come in the house. It's a lot warmer in the house."

"Oh, no thanks."

"I know how you feel about Wendy White," Marie says. But she doesn't. Flynn hates Wendy White. Flynn despises Wendy White. Flynn wishes Wendy White had never been found.

"Okay. Well, the laundry room door is open, so…" Marie pats her on the leg and gets out of the car.

*

"We're working closely with the cops, but it's kinda funny you know cause a"

"'Cause a lot of us were like, this is gonna change our."

"gonna change our life style having them around. Y-"

"around. Y'know it's like, man! They're here again we gotta put the b-"

"here again we gotta put the bong away, but they're like—it's cool, we've got something m-"

" s'cool, we've got something more important to-"

*

Sometime around morning White actually shows up. White as a ghost. She is wearing a brown miniskirt, an orange turtleneck sweater and a cheap Timex watch with a faux-leather band. It has a broken second hand that lopes its way between the numbers, moving only when it wants.

White sits in the front passenger side seat and turns to look at Flynn. She looks as she did in her 'missing' photograph and not as she did at four p.m. the previous afternoon.

"Hey Wendy," Flynn says, resigned now to her own collapse. She starts to laugh and so does Wendy White, though she doesn't look like she gets it. She looks like she is imitating Flynn, trying to copy her mannerisms because she's forgotten how the living act. Flynn stops laughing abruptly and so does White. The hair on the back of Flynn's neck turn to ice. There should be nothing mysterious about Wendy. Flynn's been researching her for months, but still the girl is horrifying. She lacks the enculturation of the living, as if she's from some strange affectless, yet familiar tribe. She stares at Flynn intensely and self-consciously runs her hands over her own face and clothes. She carries with her the faint smell of her decomposition, the odor of her death. She smiles and her teeth are gray.

"Hey Flynn," says Wendy, seeming to remember a phrase from her life. "Wanna get a beer up at Anacones?"

"Nah," says Flynn, "I'm planning on staying in this car. Anacones is great though, it's nothing against the place." They sit there quietly for a while and then Flynn says, "Y'know, Anacones patronage is emblematic of the demographic shift in the Northeast."

Wendy shrugs. "Oh, yeah?" she responds politely.

"Yeah, it is," Flynn tells her, relieved to be in command of the conversation. "Fucking Bailey Avenue is moving two blocks this way every year." It seemed like an appropriate thing to tell someone in White's improbable state. "You go cross there and it's suddenly World Health Organization territory, man. It's welcome to Beirut, El Mozote, South Central. You know what the rate of gunshot fatality is over there?"

"No."

"In the African American and Slavic population it increases by thirty percent every year. And it's what? November now? There've been ninety-four firearms-related deaths so far this year and twelve deaths related to arson."

She hopes discussing the murder rate will make White less self-conscious, and less terrifying. But White doesn't seem to care, so she just stops talking and goes back to sitting uncomfortably, looking at her breath.

"Well," says Wendy, "lets go over to Essex Street then."

"Oh yeah, great. That's a *good* one. And what'd you do the day they dug you up? Oh, I went out to the Essex Street Pub. Fucking brilliant."

White shrugs again, "I just think you should leave the car is all." Her flat drawl is beginning to grate on Flynn and she wonders if there's an implicit threat somewhere in the sentence. She starts weeping again—out of irritation this time, frustration at not being left alone. She doesn't *want* to ask White any questions. They've all been answered by that dismembered mummy, in a summer print dress, which stared up from a cut in the earth swallowing the whole world. Wendy's even more inconsequential now that she's been found. No mystery there—a crack, a hole and everything's exposed. Inside is out and neither had a hold on the other, as it turns out.

Finally, because Wendy won't leave and because Flynn's curious she asks, "Was it *just* Roberts and Mike Bectel?"

"Yeah," says Wendy dully. "Some of us from Buff State were sitting out front of the Essex partying."

Flynn detests the word "partying" and she winces when Wendy White says it. Flynn hates most euphemisms and sees them as a sign of mental and psychological weakness. Flynn wants White to say, "we were sitting out front snorting lines of cocaine," or "At one a.m. we were sitting out front drinking beer and talking." There was no "party" anywhere, despite the recent graduation. They were simply three people with associate degrees getting fucked up, and, she knows from interviews, talking about television, strip clubs over the bridge in Fort Erie, Canada, and the new Pearl Jam album. The word "partying" replaces her fear with a genuine sense of relief that White is dead. If Wendy White's death means Roberts and Bectel spend twenty years in prison getting ass fucked, that's okay with Flynn. If Wendy White is gone, if there are fewer women like White and fewer men like Roberts and Bectel every year, that's okay with Flynn. Fewer "partiers," fewer Canisius High School boys in their polo shirts with their baseball caps on backwards.

"Afterwards, we went to the Elmwood Steakout and then back to Mike's. He had this little boxer puppy and it had shit all over the place and it really stunk and we were kinda laughing about that and then BAM! My face started bleeding, from like, nowhere, and then BAM, y'know, *again*. And I was like, oh fuck. Oh no. This was really a mistake. And as I was falling down I remember thinking, I'm going to die and the last thing I'm gonna smell is dog shit."

Flynn sighs and nods impatiently.

"But it wasn't," Wendy says brightly. "It was pine and mud, like camping smells. 'Cause I was almost still alive when they buried me. Or maybe I smelled those smells today, when I first saw you. Man, you were sick, Flynn. I've never seen anyone get *that* sick."

Flynn wants White out of the car now but doesn't know how to say it. She's pissed at the girl for traumatizing her with her corpse, making her sit there in the car for eighteen hours, and also for making her hate her own nickname: 'Mighty Flynn.' Now when people say 'Mighty Flynn' it'll be sarcasm because Mighty Flynn *did* throw up uncontrollably at the site. 'Mighty Flynn' couldn't even breathe. She had Vicks on her upper lip and a handkerchief that the cop had given her to put over her mouth and she could barely breathe, so constricted was her chest. She couldn't write a word.

At twenty-three Flynn is no Joan Didion. She will never become a correspondent. Flynn is no Dorothy Day, no Amelia Earhart. Flynn will never ever be a war reporter. She couldn't even drive home afterwards because, thankfully, her car was frozen shut, and she had to call Joe for a ride. He took her back to the office to write the piece, and then drove her home. But she wouldn't get out of the car. So he took her back to his place. When it became obvious she wouldn't leave the car, he got her a few blankets and went inside.

Flynn has turned to dust in the back of an '87 Chevy parked in her editor's driveway on Lisbon avenue, round the corner from Northside Co-op. Around the corner from Anacones and it's fucking cold in that car. Colder now that White's ghost showed up. She's no Joan Didion. She threw up in front of the policemen.

"It's okay," White told her, but the ghost was wearing Flynn's disgust and distress on her face as she said it. She was even trying to mess her hair up so it looked like Flynn's.

"Just…can you, just…cut it out, for now, Wendy?"

"You're a *woman*," the ghost told her, like she was trying to re-member vocabulary, trying to break things down before she went on her way. "You're a woman. Like I was. Like *me*. Like *I* was." She looks glassy-eyed at Flynn's breath pouring from her lips in the cold car and opens her dark mouth, but nothing comes out.

*

Flynn's body makes the fourth or fifth twist down into the con-crete manger of the half pipe. The point of upside-down waiting is the period at the end of the sentence. And she skates, sentence after sentence, rolling back down and up, down and up, waiting weight-less again—the top of her head facing the cement. She wears cut-off levis and a man's ribbed undershirt, no bra, combat boots with no socks. And she's shaved one side of her head with dog clippers. One of her knees is badly brush burned. When she sees pictures of this time period she recognizes only her eyes, and she's amazed that she would walk around essentially bare breasted without giving a thought to it. Underwear was uncomfortable, who really cared? Not Flynn, she wanted to be a skater, she wanted to read books and drink beer, and play in the driveway all summer, coasting and sweating, and still at fifteen, climbing the trees and up on to the roof. Still at fifteen, building forts, stealing peoples lawn ornaments, eating candy. She developed an articulate, yet filthy vocabulary. She had sex with her boyfriend in the attic when her parents were gone, and read Fitzgerald and T. S. Eliot out loud afterwards, surrounded by boxes of mildewed books, saved schoolwork and broken furniture.

Sometimes she'd swim alone in the river, which was muddy and swollen and had silt and stones at the bottom. She wished White could have that summer. Could not wear the miniskirt and broken watch. But then the idea of White sitting at a table with two preppie boys as they talked about the best place to see money stick to naked human skin, makes her hate the dead girl all over again. *Why* did White sit there with them, at the edge of her grave? Why the fuck had she been there at all?

*

"*living room floor. Further investigation showed that they were trying to r—*"

"*gation showed that they were trying to remove a dark stain with the approximate surface area of four by four and a half feet. At this point officer Maitland and myself—*"

"*a dark stain with the approximate surface area of four by four and a half feet. At this point officer Maitland and myself informed Mr. Bectel and Mr. Roberts of—*"

"*land and myself informed Mr. Bectel and Mr. Roberts of their Miranda rights and proceeded to—*"

*

Flynn knows now that she has caught a chill. The sky is pale pink in the East and the windows of the car are covered with frost on the outside and little beads of ice caused by condensation on the inside. She sits up and catches the reflection in the rearview mirror. The

Kullman's salt-and-pepper cattle dog is sitting staring into it. He's looking at her reflection as she looks at his in the Chevy's square and frosty mirror.

"I've always hated you," the dog says when he realizes she is looking at him.

"Great," says Flynn. "I'm the motherfucking son of Sam now."

The dog doesn't know what she means and continues staring at her. "I could tell you didn't like me because I liked to catch coins. It's hard to catch coins and you don't appreciate it."

"No, Gus. I don't."

"I would bring you a quarter and you would flip it for me once or twice maybe four times but that was it. I liked to catch it and you didn't like to throw it. I like to feel it hit my teeth. I like the feel of it, when it hits my teeth. It was thin between my teeth. When it hits my teeth I like it. And when you would stop flipping the coin I wanted to bite you because I wanted you to feel my teeth too and then maybe you would understand how they feel. I wanted you to *feel* my teeth. I wanted to bite your arm but I didn't because Joe smelled like that shouldn't happen. But if you stop flipping the coin for me again, one day I will let you feel them. They are what makes me a dog."

"I've got teeth too, you fucking moron. What makes you a dog is your four legs and your tail and the fact that you can't read and I could go on and on about what else makes you a dog, but I seriously doubt you'd understand it."

"You don't know how it is," Gus says.

"No," Flynn says. "I don't. I don't know what it is to be a *dog* and I don't care. You are an annoying dog. And your mind is shot because of your coin-catching fixation."

"I hate everyone like you," says the dog. "I hate you. You don't understand about the teeth. Come out of the car now so I can eat you before anyone wakes up."

Flynn rolls her eyes at the dog's reflection in the mirror.

"Do you see how you've just told me that you will eat me and *then* told me to get out of the car? Now. Why would I leave the car if I know you are going to eat me?"

"Oh," says the dog.

"Yeah," says Flynn. "Oh." And she blows her nose on part of her shirt.

*

A rap on the window at eight a.m. and it's Gabe, her editor's oldest son, with a steaming mug of coffee. Clouds are moving rapidly across the sky above him. The gray is being replaced with an intense clear blue, and the frozen condensation on the windshield has been illuminated, and shines in the sun, beaming hundreds of circles of light into the car's interior. He smiles at her, his cheeks are red.

"We're going sledding down to Chestnut Ridge you wanna come? It's a perfect day. Well, anyway," he says before she can answer, "we're taking this car 'cause Mom's using the other one to go to bingo at Immaculate, so…."

Around ten the three little kids push into the back next to her and Joe and the two older boys get in the front after tying the toboggan to the roof.

The Chevy cruises along like a boat in a sea of ice and concrete. It's a forty-minute drive to Chestnut Ridge through the flat majesty of Great Lakes industrial land, through the bright sky and massive buildings and hilless hints of water that made Flynn want to settle there in the first place. The twins stare at her while they drive until Sarah whispers something to them.

The crest is long and steep. It shines, a sparkling white slope overlooking steel mills and granaries and ships on the cracked and partially frozen river. The river that Flynn knows contains eight thousand pounds of mercury and thirteen thousand pounds of sulfur dioxide dumped by Buffalo Dye and Color in less than a decade. Flynn knows one hundred million families like the one in this car will fall out of the middle class this year, and the United States lost over three thousand independent newspapers in less than five years. Prospects don't look good for the Kullmans, given these statistics. Particularly as they live in the city's Northeast where asthma rates among those under eighteen increased by twenty-eight percent this past summer and the concern over other diseases caused the city to hire forty-five new exterminators to tackle the rat problem. "Rat free in '93" was the made up slogan around the office. But then again, those kids played a lot of chess and went to a Catholic school and their parents let them try to dig a moat around the house despite problems with the utility companies.

Flynn is trying to hold it together with the details. The names and dates and times. The locations and the descriptions of these locations that will bring things together in a neat package, the who what when where. The facts that will prevent White's corpse from winning. White's corpse gets the Pulitzer! Gets the last word! That discarded doll of her, zipped into a bag and hoisted onto a stretcher, and driven through the snowy city in an ambulance that can take its time. She's got it now, the envy of all humanity. Not only is she a woman, she's also dead. There goes White to accept her award! Leaving Flynn, a shrinking figure on the snow's crust, pulling at her car door, and trying, periodically to blow the smells of menthol and entropy out of her sinus cavities. *I knew where they'd find you*, Flynn thinks to the back of the ambulance doors. *The foundation is laid in the details. Take my pen, take my laptop, take my tape recorder. I'll switch places with you!* She thinks to the gray skin. *I'd've known by the details, Wendy. I'd've known.*

As her work at the paper became more automatic, she remembers thinking that she was like a bricklayer.

But "Nah," Joe told her. "It's more like being a ball player—it's just that you're the ringer right now—you been hittin it outta the park a lot these days and we all like that. But even that's no big deal 'cause you always get to do it again even if you fuck up, it's just *words*. It's just newsprint, Flynn. People throw it away almost immediately. It ain't no fucking brick wall. People line their bird cages with your story. And there's no *way* I'll pay you as much as a bricklayer gets. You're a *para*grapher. You'll burn out one of these years and I'll have to rotate you over to the pussy department to write about plays or something, that's a little more like having a trade. But bricklayer? Nobody writes that good. Not even the Mighty Flynn, I'm not kidding. I'm not." He didn't say it with anything but affection, and that weird, proud uneasy look he had with her, like he was going to laugh, but didn't, out of respect.

The parking lot is enclosed by pine trees and the Kullmans pile out of the car. Their black hair and pale faces float above their scarves and coats, blowing white steam from chapped lips.

Joe pulls the hood of his Carhartt up and begins unlashing the toboggan from the roof of the car.

He and the boys carry it under their arms, walking single file towards the cabin that rests in the snow next to the toboggan run. The smaller kids get out and then after a few minutes, Flynn gets out too and walks behind the ten-year-old twins.

She's not dressed for it, she has no hat or mittens and her hair, now greasy, is plastered against her face.

She walks up the long ladder of the toboggan run behind them, but they are waiting at the top so that she can be the first one on—crossed legs tucked up beneath the curve of the sled. From the top of the run she can see the Bethlehem Steel plant like a vast, black fenced-in city, like the castle they long to see from their feudal homes, but rarely glimpse. Smoke pours from the stack into the white-gray air. And she has no words for it, no statistics on what the stack is putting out. Just the sight of its majestic expanse in her view as they race down the run.

The bodies of the Kullmans are warm at her back and her stomach is hollow with sensation and speed. Her face stings. Sarah is in the very back and sandwiched between them are all the boys. They scream together as one voice. And the printed word is gone, gone, erased by the velocity and the snow. And it's like the half pipe, only better and faster, and no slow-motion waiting. And they sing on the sled and scream. They sing "Why can't I get just one kiss? Why can't I get just one kiss? Maybe somethings I wouldn't miss but..."

In the car for a full forty minutes, damp and exhilarated from the sledding, they continue to sing. The voices of the twins, their clear vibrato-less soprano and the voices of Jesse and Gabe, a sing-song baritone and then Joe's bass. And then her own smoker's alto together with Sarah's, the lowest common denominator. The mordant report that holds it all together. That narrow range hitting those same notes again and again. Holding on in the middle, precise and clear, to that single diesis that is somehow never heard. They sing.

"Add it up! Add it up! Add it up!"

THE YOUNG GUARD

The boy is wearing thick elastic bracelets. They fit snugly around his wrists, and reach half-way up to his elbows. Black and gray. They are casings from abandoned artillery shells that he has found by the fence. He used his hands and a nail to pull them off, then pried loose the caps of the shells and collected the black gunpowder into a pile, trying not to scrape up too much dust from the ground, because it would burn better if there wasn't much dust. His friend Itai had some matches and the boy would ask him for them tonight when they were all back in their bunks. He'd borrow them so he wouldn't have to bring Itai back to his gunpowder pile. He didn't want the other kids stealing his gunpowder. Eventually he'd need a box or a bag to keep it in, but he could find that somewhere.

Right now the boy stands, dazed, on a mountain of broken concrete, looking somewhere out at the distant fields. He wears baggy jeans and a red, white and blue Evil Knievel T-shirt. Hair down to his shoulders, sweaty and full of dirt. Around his neck are thin strands of left-over ball chain from his father's tags. He breathes through his mouth; his cheeks are flushed. He pokes a stick absently into the crumbling cement. It's hot and the smell of cow shit and dust is rising from the ground, rising from the stables behind him, on the far side of the fence.

After a while he knows he's been looking at nothing for a long time and then the fields come into focus. Yellow, green, and brown squares divided by gray roads. The sky is growing orange, and the transports are coming back up the hillside. He freezes, stops poking at the ground. He remembers something and spits over the side of the broken-up bunker he's been standing on. Points the stick out at the road and closes one eye. "Stupid, stupid, stupid." He whispers, "stupid, stupid, stupid." He has remembered that his father is not down in the fields at all. His father is not driving up for dinner and will not be picking him up along the way. And this is the third time he has made this mistake. "Teh-teh teh-teh teh-teh," he says beneath his breath, pointing the stick at the slow transports. "Boom. Drachhhh. Teh-teh teh-teh teh-teh," He stands until the sky is all dark red and then purple. It's a long time to wait for nothing.

The boy's father was American, but he spoke no English. Said he didn't even want to hear that language. And he especially didn't want to hear his boy speak it. So the boy didn't. He only faked it when anyone asked if he knew it. He could make a convincing R sound and he could make the TH sound. And he could sing 'Take a Walk on the Wild Side' along with his father's album. His father had no accent. He spoke like an Israeli. Better than an Israeli, because he used words that were more proper. Older words. His father had long hair like the boy's but he'd shaved it all close to his head before he left. He had smooth dark skin and dark eyes and smoked cigarettes that came in an all-white box. He wore a shirt from his school in America with those letters that go backwards. UCLA, it said. The boy could read it, and he could find those same letters in books his father had.

The boy had already turned six while his father was gone. And he knew that his father had also had a birthday in that time. This is what the gunpowder was for. And the bracelets. And also several drawings of the cotton sprayer, and the inside of a cowboy's house, which he was saving under the couch in his mother's apartment. But the gunpowder was really the best, and he had a perfect, quiet spot picked out, a flat stretch of sidewalk to set it up. He imagined the letters. Before he had found the second box of buried ammunition he was planning on writing "Aba" but now he would spell out his father's entire name. It would be a surprise.

When his father came back he would work again in the cotton, and he would take his boy with him on the weekends. They would drive down together in the jeep, and eat salad for breakfast on the bench outside the storage shed. Just like they did every weekend before the war.

He kicked some stones free from the concrete and decided to get moving before it was too dark. He didn't know if the lights would be on tonight or not, and he didn't like to follow the glow in the dark stripes painted on the walkway by himself. He didn't want to end up in the wrong shelter, get stuck with grown-ups. He wanted to go to the children's shelter, so they could stay up and play marbles.

The children's shelter was harder to find in the dark. That thought always makes him feel hurried and excited around this time of evening so he thinks it again, to see if the hair on his arms would stand up a second time.

Nevermind. He can see the light of the main dining hall already turned on. And the boys from his group are walking together; the young guards, the young workers, in their dark blue shirts. He runs across the dust road, he jumps the trench instead of crossing on the boards, then feels the cushion of the sod lawn just as he falls in line with them. Puts his arm around Itai's shoulders, and the two of them look down to see if they are walking in step with eachother. Itai smiles up at the boy. Then raises his eyebrows.

"You should go get your shirt," he tells him.

"Why? What?"

"Go put on your blue shirt."

"No. It's okay like this."

"Come with me," he says, taking the boy's hand. "We'll run back to school and get your shirt." Itai turns and runs, pulling the boy by the wrist, jerking him around. The boy is the youngest in his group, the only six year old, but he is not the smallest. Itai is seven and several inches taller than the boy, but somehow slighter. They race hand in hand past the other groups. Trying to get ahead of each other but not letting go. They burst in the door of the empty children's house. It's dark and chilly in the room. Their low rubber boots make hollow echoing squeaking sounds on the tile as they scuff around in the dark. Their eyes adjust and they can make out the bunk beds and bookcases. Hanging down from the light chain in the center of the room is a yellow matchbox tractor. The boy yanks it and floods the white-tiled room with fluorescent light. Itai jumps up and sits on the dresser to wait. The boy's drawer is the third one down and he opens it; there is nothing in it but the blue shirt. He opens Itai's drawer out of curiosity. There is nothing in it at all.

"Is it laundry?" he asks

Itai shrugs.

The boy grabs the blue shirt and pulls it on over Evil Knievel.

"Have you still got those matches?" he asks.

Itai shakes his head and makes a short sucking sound behind his top teeth.

"Hasn't your mother any matches at her apartment?" the boy asks him.

"Yeah. Hasn't *your* mother?"

"She doesn't smoke."

"She doesn't *smoke*?"

"She doesn't. When you go visit, get the matches, okay?"

"What for?"

"And I will show you where to dig for shells, okay?

"Okay, okay, o*kaaay*," he yells, jumping down from the dresser. He pulls the light chain and grabs the boy's wrist again.

They run out the door and across the lawn to the dining room. They race to the heavy wooden door and heave it open. The room is full. All the young guards are there. Five year olds on up. The high-school group sits smoking near the door, long-haired boys and their girlfriends, in their blue shirts and flared jeans and clogs. The boy's group is already seated in the back of the dining room beneath the framed photographs of their grandparents; standing bespectacled in gray tank tops, leaning on shovels and picks near a pile of rocks. Itai and the boy stop running and walk to the table, sliding into their seats.

Avi leans into the table to pour water for their group. "They're coming back," he says. "That's why we're here with the shirts."

The boy feels sick, a shock to his stomach, and he can feel his heart beating. He snaps his bracelets against his wrist under the table, one by one so they sting his arm. He looks up at the picture of his mother's father standing in an empty field of mud. That's where the sewing shop is now. Where all that dirt was.

"A whole unit of fighters from here. They're probably with our mothers right now, waiting to come in and see us."

"A whole unit of *what*?" asks the boy, and he makes Avi's voice say "paratroopers," inside his head.

"A unit from the front," Avi says, pushing his glasses up on his face. The boy hates him with every word that he speaks. "I heard someone say 'a whole unit,' and I think that's what they're talking about."

Avi's father had come home last month, picked him up from school still wearing his uniform, and *carried* him home. He *carried* him. An *eight* year old, like a baby. The next day they caught Avi by the fish pond and made him fight Itai. His lips bled and they called him a baby for getting beat by a seven year old, and they threw his glasses out in the grass. They would have thrown them in the pond but he was their friend.

"What front?"

"I don't know."

"You don't know anything," the boy told him. "We're probably here to learn how to take rifles apart."

"We don't do rifles until the first day of the week," Avi tells him matter of factly. Avi's not mad at anyone.

"Paratroopers," the boy whispers to himself. He wants to say it out loud for good luck so he says "Paratroopers are the toughest fighters," to no one in particular.

"*All* of them are the toughest fighters," Itai says, repeating something their teacher tells them to break up fights. The boys laugh.

"She looks like a boiled mouse," Levi says of their teacher.

"A boiled, puking mouse," says Ahlon.

"No, but, no, but … Paratroopers," the boy says, "have M-16s and and M-16s are better than uzis."

"Not true," Levi says.

"True," says the boy. "Uzi is not a good gun. And it's not a big gun." He snapped his bracelets under the table to the rhythm of the national anthem.

"They are *all* good guns," Itai says sarcastically.

The conversation makes the boy feel better because it is part of a routine, part of a daily debate. It gives him the opportunity to steadfastly defend M-16s, and to take pride in knowing that he has never changed his mind on the subject. He drinks his cup of water. He feels that at any minute his father's unit will walk in the door. And his father and Itai's father will come over to their boys and pick them up. And take them home. And let them sleep on the couch in their parents' apartments for the special occasion.

The boy could picture his father walking across the lawn in his sneakers and jeans with a cigarette tucked in the corner of his mouth. No, he would be too excited to be smoking, or to have even changed his clothes. He would be running in his fatigues; he would tell the boy's mother he could see her later, and then he would run straight to the children's house to look for the boy. When he wouldn't find him he would rush to the dining room, before everyone else. He would look quickly around the room and spot his son at once. He would open his arms and the boy would jump down from his chair and run to him. And they would walk out together, before the other soldiers came. Before they had to sing "The Internationale." They would take a long walk and the boy would carry his father's gun for him. Finally they would see his mother, and she would say: "You look even more like your father now that you're six. You look exactly like him."

Levi's aunt, a high school teacher, stands up in the front of the dining room. And holds up her hand.

"Shalom, yeladim. We are here to go over the rules for extended stay in shelters. When we finish up here you will go to your parents' apartments overnight. Tomorrow we will begin what may be a long stay in the shelters. All of your things have been packed. Each children's group will have a high school leader. We will be underground where it is very safe and comfortable." Levi's aunt smiles broadly at them, "I want you now to look around at your friends." She gestures with her hands, raising them up high again.

They look at each other, look across the room. It is a sea of blue shirts and dark hair.

"Now look at your own group," she says.

The boy and Itai turn their heads to look at each other.

"Good," she says. She is proud of them.

The boy knows that now she will ask them to sing. He snaps his bracelets and cracks his knuckles. They sing. When it's time for questions Itai asks if they have already packed his bag of marbles. Levi's aunt smiles again, says "Yes, they have."

*

His mother has made cake.

Like in a dream, she says the very words he had imagined earlier "…now that you are six."

She wears boots, blue pants and a white shirt. Sits across the table from him watching him eat cake and drink watery, red fruit punch. Spring is a bad time for allergies, he thinks looking at her face. She smiles at him and wipes her nose.

"…your pajamas, okay?"

He shoves the second piece of cake into his mouth and it makes her laugh.

"…okay, honey?" She reaches out to him and he climbs into her lap with his mouth full.

"….gets home and we'll…"

He shuts his eyes.

"…maybe by the time…"

She brushes his hair back from his forehead.

"…swimming and then go see the…"

He can't listen to her. He can only feel her and smell her clean clothes. He curls deeper into her lap, rests his head on her chest. She stands up and carries him into the bathroom, turns on the shower without putting him down. She puts the lid of the toilet down and sits, holding him while the steam from the shower floats slowly from around the curtain.

"Arms up," she says, and he lifts his arms above his head while she pulls off the shirts. She sets him down in front of her, and he takes off his jeans, climbs back into her lap naked. He is pale, ashkanazi, and his hair curls at the ends.

At the children's house they all take showers together in the evening. And no one dresses or undresses them. The bathroom is getting warmer and he feels tired. He wouldn't want Itai or Ahlon seeing him now, sitting on his mother's lap.

She pulls back the curtain and puts him down under the warm water. She kneels beside the shower, reaches in and washes his back with a soapy washcloth. Runs her hands over his hair and then scrubs it for a long time with yellow shampoo. He can feel her fingernails on his scalp. She washes his dirty hands and wrists, rubbing soap over his bracelets to clean the dust out of them. The water running into the drain is gray. She stands up and leans by the shower, wiping her long wet hair away from her face.

"Is a whole unit coming home?" he asks her.

"No," she says. "Not yet."

"I heard a whole unit of paratroopers is coming home," he tells her from behind the curtain.

"Hm," she says.

"They'll come first to the children's house," he says.

"That's right," she says. "When they do come home, that's where they'll go."

He watches the gray water whirling down the drain. Puts his foot over it to make the water fill up the bottom of the shower. She brings his pajamas and a towel into the bathroom and sits waiting for him to get out. She dries him off and hands him his pajamas. And then gets clean sheets out of the hall closet and hands them to him. He unfolds them on the couch, walking to either end to tuck them in. She has a big pillow that she sets on one side of the couch for him. She pats the sheets and he climbs inside and rests his head. She throws the duvet over him, and then lies next to him brushing his clean damp hair back. His skin is soft and his cheeks are white beneath the light of the gooseneck lamp. Her voice is quiet. He's cozy in the apartment now that the couch is set up and his feet are off the cold tile.

"…used to see *rabbits* running through the …"

"…and your grandfather said…"

"…a letter soon…"

"…visit Haifa and see the boats that…"

He lays on his side and counts the black-and-gold papier-maché demitasse cups on the kitchen shelf across from the couch. He wraps his arm around her neck.

"…in the morning, okay?"

She kisses him.

"Okay?"

She turns off the light.

His eyes are unfocused. The apartment is silent and warm. She watches him lose consciousness, from the archway that separates her bedroom from the other room. Just before he falls asleep his body jerks suddenly, his fingers stiffen. His eyes open, then slowly slide shut and he breathes out, already asleep.

*

The boy pulls down the bunks that hang from the side of the cement wall; they swing out on their hinges and stop on their chains.

"Top bunk!" Ahlon yells.

The boy climbs up and throws himself down on the top before Ahlon can. Ahlon stands on the bottom bunk and grabs the boy's feet. He kicks free.

"I called top bunk,"

"I'm *in* the top bunk," the boy tells him.

"I'm in the top bunk tomorrow," says Ahlon.

"Go to the other wall and get theirs," the boy whispers down at him.

Ahlon crosses the narrow air raid shelter and pulls the bunks down on the other side. He climbs to the top, and he and the boy smile at each other from their spots near the ceiling.

Sagulite and Shira are playing cards with Itai, sitting cross-legged on the floor. Shira is still talking about her dog and how when she turns eight she will work in the horse stables with her mother.

"You can bring your dog with you in the stables," she says.

"Big deal," Itai says. "You can bring your dog with you anywhere."

"You can't bring him if you're in the sewing shop," she tells him severely.

Levi and Yarden are reading, lying on their stomachs on sleeping bags.

Their group leader is telling the rest of them a story, in between drags of his cigarette. He wears a long-sleeved white T-shirt and blue work pants and clogs. His hair is long, tightly curled black ringlets. He's thin and muscular.

He has brought a stack of books to read to them, but now he's telling them about the last day of induction into the Young Guard. He tells them when they turn ten, they'll go together, just their group, with their backpacks, and they'll follow a map to a place outside the fence ten kilometers from here.

Itai looks up at the group leader and back at the girls playing cards. "They want us to hike to Lebanon," he jokes. And the girls laugh.

"The map has only numbers instead of places," the group leader continues. And the numbers tell you what kind of landscape you're looking at, whether it's a hill or a lake or a group of trees. If you read it wrong you can get off course for a long time."

"Did your group read it wrong?"

"We read it wrong all the time. They gave us one backpack that had all the water and food in it for the whole group and we gave it to one guy to carry, and because we got lost a couple of times, he got really really mad, carrying all the heaviest things. Who could blame him? So we divided up the food and water and everybody carried some of the heavy things. We walked in a big circle and that's how we figured out our mistake with the map. And then we got there."

"Where?"

"I can't tell you," he whispered to them smiling. "It's a secret place."

The boy leans over the side of the bunk to listen better.

"After we finished that hike we were really a part of the movement."

"We're *all* part of the movement," Itai says. He wants everyone to laugh but they are listening. Ignoring him.

"We went on much longer hikes every summer after that. Fifteen- and twenty-kilometer hikes, and down south in the desert. They were the best because it was so quiet and the sky was not like it is here at all. And this is the reason we're the best." He raises his eyebrows and nods at the children. "This is the reason *we* are the most respected. If you come from the city you don't know how to do *anything*. You don't know how to hike or read maps or any of the little things, things that your group already knows how to do, like hide or track or find water. Think about what it would be like to be eighteen years old and not know how to find water. All of you know how to do these things before you go to the army, and all of your fathers knew how to do these things before they went, too. And that's why we can go into dangerous places and not get killed."

The boy stares down at the group leader. His stomach hurts. He hangs his arms over the side of the bunk and snaps at his bracelets. Yawns. He stares at the mural painted on the gray wall above the low thick metal door. It's a picture of tropical fish and coral and sea anemones.

"And that's why we can win against enemies who are so big." They are all listening now. The group leader continues, smiles at them. "Because we *know* how to work together and we *know* how to fight hard."

"What are you going to be?" Shira asks him.

"If I pass the written test, I'll be a pilot. If the war is still going on next year when I am eighteen, I'll be some kind of fighter."

"Fighter," the boy whispers, rolls onto his back. It's cold and the walls feel slightly damp. It's like camping. He jumps off the bunk and almost lands on Levi. The bottoms of his feet sting from landing so hard. He pushes into the card game and takes seven cards off the top of the pile for his hand. Itai is happy to have him play and he pushes the boy over and wrestles him around on the floor a little. The boy is laughing. He pushes Itai away, gets up and sits cross-legged, close to his friend, so their knees touch. When it's Sagulite's turn, he whispers into Itai's ear.

"Have you got the matches?"

Itai puts his arm around the boy's shoulders and looks at him out of the corners of his eyes. He presses his lips tightly together and nods in confidence.

*

When the bombing is over, Levi's aunt comes and opens the doors, with her proud smile. She pats the group leader on the back sympathetically. She tells them to pack up their things and put all the laundry in a pile inside the door of the children's house. They rush past her up the steps without their things.

"Okay," she says, "so you'll do it later." She grabs Levi on his way past her and squeezes his face and kisses him. He squints, hops impatiently, and she lets him go.

It is late afternoon and they run out onto the sod lawn and jump over the trench back and forth and back and forth. Itai and the boy run to the shed outside the children's house to get bikes. They ride first around the dirt road that circles the dining room, and then race along, uphill, standing up to pedal, to the edge of the fence. They ride all the way to the front gate and stop on the crumbling bunker to rest. Beneath them the fields look very different, as if they'd already been harvested. And there are craters in the road. They only look for a short time before riding again, coasting down the big hill to Itai's mother's apartment. She's not there, so they eat all the sugar cubes in the bowl on the table. The boy looks in the closet for a plastic bag and finding one, stuffs it into his pocket. Itai takes a plastic bag and rummages in the cupboard for more sugar. He pours half the sugar cubes quickly from their green box into the bag and then they leave again, to coast around.

The boy takes Itai to a field beyond the stables near the northernmost edge of the fence and shows him where he's been digging. Just below the surface, the ground is full of shells from mortars and artillery, rounds for automatic weapons, and bullets for rifles. Itai picks up handfuls of bullets and laughs, opens his eyes wide. They push everything they can find into one pile and divide it up. The boy puts his rounds into the bag; he will carry them back to his gunpowder pile later and take them apart.

Itai is pulling the casings off the mortar rounds and twisting them around his wrist. He holds it up and the boy holds his arm up next to Itai's to compare.

"Don't tell anyone else," the boy says. "Or just don't tell Avi, but you can tell Shira and Ahlon."

Itai nods. He gives the boy a box of matches and he takes out his own box. He pries the cap off of a bullet and spills out a tiny black pile and then sets it on fire. It hisses and a thin line of smoke rises straight up. He pries off another and makes the letter Alef on the ground in gunpowder and sets the edge of it on fire. The flame travels quickly around the letter and burns out.

"Wah *a*lla," he says. "It's nice."

The boy nods, smiles. "Yeah, it's nice."

"We can find a way to fire those mortars," Itai says.

"If we ask older boys, they'll know how, but they'll take our stuff." They look at one another gravely. They want badly to set off some of the rounds.

"We can say we just found a couple and then they can show us how," Itai says. "If they take just a couple from us, I bet they'll let us watch."

The boy nods. "Okay, we'll do it tomorrow. I have to go check something," he says, tying his plastic bag to the handlebars of the bike. He rides further down along the edge of the fence, whistling, looking back once to see Itai crouching above a bright little fire.

*

One full bag of gunpowder with string tied in triple knots around the top. One half box of matches. Five drawings. He is thoroughly washed and he kicks his feet against the legs of the chair. Snaps the elastic at his wrists. He is six and a half and he knows that his father is now thirty-two.

"Is he thirty-two or thirty-two and a half?" he asks his mother.

She laughs. She has been laughing all day at everything he says. She smiles at him and doesn't answer, flips through a magazine.

"Thirty-two or thirty-two and a half?"

"Mmm?" she looks up at him as if he had never said anything. Then she says, "Thirty two."

"I'm going out to play," he tells her.

She smiles so widely at him with her eyes so shiny that he stares at her in suspicion. She laughs again.

"What are you looking at? Go ahead," she tells him. "Go!"

The sky is a clear, bright blue and they all have off from school for the afternoon.

He goes straight to his bag of gunpowder and begins to lug it over to the enclosed flat stretch of sidewalk by his mother's door. It's heavier than it looks and he is already sweaty and dirty again by the time he gets it to the spot. He sits down in the sun and rests his bent arm over his head, squinting. It smells like flowers outside the house and the banana tree in the front yard looks even bigger and sloppier than it did last year; its trunk a stringy mess. He gazes up as a helicopter makes a low pass over the group of one-story stucco duplexes that make up the entire neighborhood. Then he turns his back to the sun and sets to work.

He pulls a small piece off the corner of the bag and begins to slowly pour out the gunpowder. He makes the first few letters. It's a strange name, with letters that usually aren't put together. He has it all written in black, not quite uniform, but you can read it.

He turns so that he can see if anyone is approaching the house, sitting in front of the gunpowder to hide it. He feels in his pocket again for his matches. Another helicopter passes. He can feel the hot sun on his hair and arms, making him sleepy. He can see the heat making the air ripple like water above the road in the distance, and hear the sounds of jeeps. People have been getting dropped off all day.

He squints and from somewhere beyond his sight a group of men step out from beneath the canvas hood of a personnel carrier. They embrace, with the straps of their rifles across their chests. With their guns still on their backs.

His father is the first to break free from the group and walk slowly toward the house. The boy is standing, though he doesn't remember getting up. He knows his father's step. Sees his shoulders square in the uniform. He stands up straight on the walkway, unable to move his feet. His father's hair has grown out and he can see from a distance that he has grown a beard. His skin looks very dark; his uniform is wrinkled and faded. His father smiles so broadly, the boy can see his teeth amidst the black hair on his face. The boy can see him taking a deep breath and running toward the house. The boy pulls out his matches and turns to the name. He lights the edge of the H and jumps gracefully back away from the fire so his father can see it. He did it.

HARRY GREENBURG it blazes, hissing and popping and sending thick black smoke into the summer sky.

"Look aba!" the boy shouts, waving his arms above his head. "I wrote your name in gunpowder!" His father races up the walk, and grabs his boy. He kneels and kisses him on the face and runs his big hands over the boy's hair, closes his fists around the fine brown curls and rests his forehead against the boy's shoulder. His father is huge and solid. Made of muscle, he looks bigger to the boy, and his arms are wide inside his dirty uniform. He smells like sweat and cigarettes. His hair is full of fine dust and the boy puts his hands in his father's beard and tries to rub it clean, puts his face against his father's and squeezes him around the neck. His father takes deep breaths and holds them. The smell of sulfur is overpowering. The separate streams of smoke that rise above each letter come together above their heads in one black column that continues to rise.

The man weeps. He clenches his eyes shut and tears fall on the boy's shirt. The boy pats his father's back and kisses his face. The man cries hard now, and whispers in English, whispers the same unintelligible words over and over again, breathing and holding his breath. Breathing and holding his son's small body to his chest.

"I wrote your *name*, aba," the boy says. "I wrote your name in gunpowder."

CHILDHOOD

It was my childhood dream to become either an alcoholic, or a very old man. After thinking it over for some time it became obvious that the latter, though it would be more difficult to achieve in the short term, would afford me more respect.

I dressed in brown corduroy pants and oxford shirts, tweed sports jackets and loafers. I kept a pack of Players navy-cut cigarettes in my breast pocket and read a lot of Ibsen. I went out regularly by myself to cafes and to plays put on at the college, for which I only had to pay a child's admission price. I bought a pair of leather slippers and a smoking jacket. Every evening I would sit in front of the television, watching *Sixty Minutes*, and drinking ice water mixed with vanilla from a scotch glass. It was a quiet life.

Later I incorporated a tweed cap and some neckties into my wardrobe; I had six or seven ties given me by my father, and had purchased another four from the Salvation Army. I had more and better quality neck ties than any other girl my age. I was also able to find a pocket watch at Goodwill for fifty cents.

I was thin and long limbed and easily mistaken for a boy. I am certain that some days, while waiting for the bus, if the light was right or if my back was turned, people thought I was indeed a little old man.

My wardrobe established, I began to listen only to swing music. And it was then I realized that I had been a music critic before my retirement. I missed my apartment in the city terribly, and also my desk in the newsroom where I had sat composing my columns, cigarette smoke catching in the orange light that came through the metal blinds. I missed my rapport with the musicians and my free passes to their performances. I missed the other writers and I especially missed Diego Rivera and his wife, whom I had met briefly when Diego was painting a mural at Rockerfeller Center. I began to wish I had never agreed to move in with my daughter and her husband, the psychologist. I did not like Upstate New York and I couldn't stand my daughter's taste in decorating, which struck me as somehow both bucolic and pretentious. But mostly I hated that my daughter referred to me as "Toots," and insisted that I attend dance lessons every single day except weekends. These dance lessons were humiliating. My class was made up of a group of ten-to-fourteen-year-old girls who dressed in pink tights and white leotards. Often I was singled out in class and placed at a small bar in the middle of the room, so these children could observe my technique. Which was, I'll admit, precise. But it was also completely uninspired. When my daughter picked me up from dance lessons she would say, "How was class, Toots?"

"I need to find some peers," I would tell her, thinking of Rivera and Kahlo, and my other friend Man Ray. "This is a strange place you've decided to settle in. Personally, I think it's a reactionary decision on your part. Certainly *I* didn't raise you to seek out the type of intellectual vacuity that exists in this town."

"I found a chain for your pocket watch, Tootsie," she said.

I took to reading all day, listening to swing music on my son-in-law's stereo with a pair of gray plastic headphones he had bought for me. My son-in-law, the psychologist, oddly referred to me as "Beauty," which says a great deal about his ability to asses reality. But then, they say that only the disturbed make good psychologists. He would come home in the evening and say, "How's my little Beauty?" And I would peer at him from over the paper and rattle the ice in my glass. I couldn't imagine how my daughter had married such a mental deficient, from such a poor and ignorant background. They were both a disappointment.

Finally I told my daughter flat out that I could no longer attend Madame Helena's School of Dance.

"She was trained in the Soviet Union," my daughter said, hoping to appeal to the party politics of the era in which I once wrote.

"I don't care," I told her. "It's humiliating. I can't wear that ridiculous costume anymore."

"But look what you wear every *day*, Toots. You look so cute in your leotards. You look so free like a little girl should."

It was this last statement that really showed what a skewed vision of the world she and her husband shared. The very idea.

"Listen," I said. "I appreciate you paying for the lessons. I realize you and your husband are only trying to make my stay here less boring. But this isn't the way. I used to take in a lot of ball games at Yankee Stadium, maybe there's some athletic program going on over at the senior center."

"You're staying in dance," she said gravely. "You've been in dance since you were a baby. You've been studying for *nine* years."

"I wouldn't exactly call it study. Maybe I could pick up some free-lance work for the local paper," I told her. And she began to cry. "I'm sorry," I said. "I can no longer cram my tired old feet into those leather and wooden torture shoes." I rattled the ice in my vanilla water nonchalantly, to show her who was the parent. I produced an excellent smokers cough, and then took a handkerchief out of the pocket of my smoking jacket and wiped my forehead with it. "I'm just too tired," I said.

When my son-in-law came home he said, "Hey, Beauty Rose, Mom said you're quitting dance."

"*Who*?" I asked him, not even bothering to set the paper down.

"What's going to happen to Daddy's little ballerina?" he asked.

I assumed that he was bringing his work home with him by speaking in such strange juxtapositions, and in such an inappropriate and disrespectful manner to his father-in-law. But then this type of psychiatric babble was his life's work and it did provide me with bus fare and spending money. I remained silent instead of giving him the comeuppance he deserved for speaking to me that way. His strange remark convinced me that he was also sexist. As a socialist I was opposed to sexism. The more I thought about it, the more I realized that this sexist had warped my not-so-bright daughter's understanding of the world. I couldn't believe she was foolish enough to anchor her identity to a man who would use the phrase "Daddy's little ballerina." It was a disgusting idea, a man owning a little ballerina.

They dropped the topic of dance and I went about my daily activities, reading and taking in plays, watching the news and drinking my vanilla water. I resigned myself to living upstate with them. I tried out different caps. I thought my only annoyance now would be my daughter's habit of cutting my sandwiches into heart shapes. This I tolerated because I had never liked crust.

With dance lessons safely in my past I had more time to read and to practice what I felt to be one of life's great joys, jumping rope. A man my age needed a certain amount of cardiovascular exercise, and since I had been a featherweight boxer in college, I had gotten used to jumping rope as part of my training. Every afternoon I would jump rope for an hour or so in my daughter's driveway. I found that singing helped pass the time while jumping so I sang some of those great American traditional songs like "Engine Engine Number Nine" and "Miss Lucy had a Steam Boat." We used to sing those songs around the office to determine who got stuck with the dull assignments. No one wanted to be O-U-T. This practice gave me a great deal of pleasure, except when it was interrupted by my daughter bringing one of her heart-shaped sandwiches down the driveway and setting it off to the side with a glass of ice tea. She usually said something insipid like, "You look so cute, Toots," or "All that jumping must be getting you hungry, Tootsie pie." I would ignore her because that kind of behavior should never be encouraged.

I also had a great deal of time to observe the interactions between my daughter and her husband. It seemed that my daughter spent her days vacuuming, doing laundry, cooking, watering plants, and rearranging furniture. Her husband would come home every evening and fall asleep on the couch, after an exhausting day of siphoning off the dysfunction of others in the community. When he awoke he would recount this dysfunction through a series of vagaries and platitudes that appeared to represent professionalism. He was like an employee of a uranium mine, coming home after digging and making his family radioactive. In reality his demeanor expressed an ego that had long gone unchecked, a martyr complex, a chauvinism, poorly developed intellectualism and misanthropy so thinly veiled I was certain he had chosen his career to exact some sense of power over his own neurosis and emptiness. Every day when he came home and they kissed in the doorway, it was *Cinderella* meets the *Emperor's New Clothes*. Cinderella whistling while she wove a mantle of false confidence for him through her own ambitionless materialism.

"Hey Beauty Rose," my son-in-law would say to me. "Who is Daddy's little girl?" I would stare blankly at him and he would laugh and shake his head. "You're always going to be Daddy's little girl no matter how big you get, you know that, don't you?" Sometimes he would stand by my daughter as she worked in the kitchen, with his arms folded across his chest and say things like, "*That*'s not the way you make vegetable stock, *is* it?" or, pointing to something just below his fingertip, "You better wipe that up." Then he would sit at the table and drum his fingers in different nonrhythmic patterns while she worked. The finger drumming sometimes led to whistling, so that all of the work being done, or in my case the reading being done, moved to a kind of counter-musical human noise, a nagging of taps and shrills that seemed meant somehow to suck all internal attention, all thought or personal contemplative pleasure, towards the rattling that radiated out from his position at the table. As a person whose musical sensibility was finely tuned, I found this nearly unbearable.

My son-in-law's need for attention put everyone around him in a constant state of interruption. My daughter did nothing about this, though I observed her annoyance. Finally one evening I looked up from my book and asked him to stop this practice. He laughed and beamed into my face with great condescending affection, "What? Don't you like Daddy's whistling?" My request seemed to bring out a great need for him to continue this behavior whenever he was home. As if it were a game we now had. Being asked to stop amused him a great deal. If you turned and tried to engage him in a productive manner, to dissuade his fidgeting he would lecture you on his favorite topic: child abuse. He would detail graphic accounts of child abuse going on nearby, but by whom he couldn't disclose. These impassioned speeches to us were a great complement to the noise in terms of intrusiveness. If you began to tell him about your day, his eyes would glaze over. He liked to lecture with a melancholic nostalgia about himself. As if he were, in fact, some poltergeist of a man that had once had enough self-possession to just be quiet.

My own daughter was not much better, but to her credit, I believe she had been driven completely insane through constant interruption and disrespect. She was, sadly, not very bright. Whenever she looked as if she were about to say something about his behavior he would tell her she was beautiful. This had a terrifically pacifying effect on her. Almost as if she had been drugged. It seemed to me she had been much brighter as a child. The only minor consolation was that, despite what they thought, they had no children of their own.

Eventually the fact that I had nowhere else to go began to wear on me. I gave up even attempting to read or ponder anything of significance when they were around for fear of interruption, and the negative feelings associated with it. I could achieve nothing now that I had moved in with them. I could feel my mind and heart beginning to atrophy. My independence and self-esteem suffered terribly. They were poor conversationalists, with little or no understanding of politics, and no genuine appreciation for beauty. I could not show them the writing that I or my friends had done, nor play them the recordings of the music I loved. I feared that doing such things would result either in my son-in-law bastardizing the work through amusical mimicry, or my daughter buying me a night shirt with a picture of Cab Calloway on it.

My financial dependence on them made me feel like some kind of scab. I hadn't felt so low since the Triangle Shirtwaist fire, when all those little girls were burned to death because the owner of the factory barred the doors shut from the outside. I longed to be put in a nursing home.

"A nursing home?" My daughter asked incredulously. "You're

eleven years old," she laughed and tugged at the brim of my cap.

Each day I would consult my pocket watch to make sure it was after twelve p.m. before I began to drink. As a newspaper man, college graduate, and former featherweight boxer, I was familiar with intoxication. Not sloppy intoxication, but the kind required to get through the type of situation I currently found myself in. A tight-lipped kind of intoxication that makes dealing with bores and anti-intellectuals either tolerable or amusing. The kind that draws you out into the big picture, so far out that you can take comfort in the idea of the sun exploding, and then everything else seems so temporary and insignificant.

I would wake up, spend several hours reading, practice my rope-jumping regimen, listen to the BBC World Service on the radio, then pour myself two shots of Grand Marnier from a large bottle I had found in the pantry. Later in the day I might have another. I also took up napping.

Meanwhile, my daughter appeared to have finally snapped. She spent more and more time in front of the mirror applying various treatments to her face. Curling her eyelashes, sucking in her cheeks, and repeating certain phrases to her reflection. She tried out different expressions. One in which she would raise an eyebrow and turn her head slightly to the left, while still meeting her own gaze, was particularly disturbing. For a while this benefited me, as she left me alone. She stopped making my sandwiches and doing my laundry. It seemed that when she was speaking to me she was trying out different voice modulations, laughs, and body postures that were meant for some invisible person. She was unable even to look at me without her strange new rehearsed face. Or the distracted look of calculating what that face's impact would be on the invisible person. Between her husband's noise and her posturing to the unseen, the house was getting very crowded.

She began to read cultural-theory books, which I took as a positive sign, until I realized that they were being used as props, and also scripts. The language in the books was used in the same way the glance in the mirror was. Only in this case, I was the mirror. In an affected voice, slightly lower than her own, with a tone of gravity and suggested world-weariness she would parrot Gloria Steinem. She seemed to have no sense of the hilarity of doing this while dressed in a see-through silk blouse purchased with her husband's credit card. Steinem as coquetry. Very attractive.

I suggested she read some Emma Goldman and she gave me a sophisticated and condescending smirk, as if she knew who Emma Goldman was. Clearly at this point in her savvy, experienced life of enduring the hardships of cooking and plant watering, she was above Emma Goldman. While I couldn't fault her for realizing that women had it bad, I had no idea how she meant to make her life, or any woman's life, better by this new behavior. I thought briefly that it might be some kind of performance art, and that my daughter was actually a genius. But that was just parental blindness, a hope that I hadn't failed completely.

I went back to reading the paper and drinking my Grand Marnier on the rocks. I had begun to time it so that I would be just intoxicated enough to tolerate my son-in-law's yammering when he arrived home. My daughter now responded to being called beautiful by her husband by acting as though she had been slapped. The loathing she had adopted for my son-in-law was completely out of proportion to anything he had actually done. And it was amazing, and also hilarious to watch, particularly after a few drinks. It was as if they were reading from a script of a Soviet propaganda play meant to instruct on the corrosive, soul-crushing, and intellect-warping evils of capitalist society.

It wasn't long before my son-in-law stopped talking to me altogether, I guess it was because I had raised his wife, and admittedly done such a poor job. But the finger tapping continued and was now coupled with an aggressive and sarcastic grimace in my direction. My daughter was not home often and no longer cooked meals for us. My son-in-law would eat on the way home from work. I would make myself spaghetti with butter and drink vanilla water or whatever wine was in the house. I still took in plays. I did my own laundry, my own shopping. I watched *Sixty Minutes*, I read. I jumped rope.

And I remembered the days when I was a writer, the orange light slanting through the metal blinds in the newsroom, singing Engine Engine Number Nine with the other staffers and going out to listen to jazz. I remembered how strong the women were, and how genuine the men. I remembered those little girls in the Triangle Shirtwaist Factory. And how we all cried down at the pub after work, the day they burned to death.

THE APIARIST

The helicopter hovered above the girl, hovered above the still green retina of the in-ground pool and the girl on her towel. A single, armed Adonis hung from the door in his flak jacket, black glasses and boots. And the girl shaded her eyes to get a better look. She hoped he might land out on the lawn, out on the long green stretch of flat land that lay between the underchlorinated pool and the perimeter fence. But the helicopter was caught as it descended, pulled up suddenly as if by an invisible wire, and then it banked just as quickly and was gone.

It was one o'clock and she was done with work. It was one hundred and four degrees and she lay sweating on her towel. The grass was hot and spikey, and she was reluctant to get up and run to the even hotter cement that surrounded the pool. Several times she almost made herself do it, but her mind wandered. She grew lazy. She rested her arm over her face and began to fall asleep. It was times like these she thought of the hive.

She thought of the bees sleeping, the bees eating in a cloud of smoke, growing drowsy in the white box, while she and Tetsuo tended to them. She was overcome now by the olfactory memory of wax and honey and smoke. And she wished she was back at work again in that different world.

A second helicopter passed lower than the first, blocking out the sun, shading the girl's face so she could open her eyes without squinting. The blades made the grass ripple and the corners of her towel flap; it was the first cool breeze all day. She pulled the top of her bathing suit down to expose her pale breasts to the cool air and to the killers that gazed out from inside the helicopter. The machine hovered and one of the soldiers leaned out to snap a picture. The other one must have been anti-personnel, she thought, and this one goes afterwards to take aerial photographs.

Up above, the boy with the gun grinned to the rest of the squad. "That was so *nice* of her," he said.

"Yeah, that's *all* Green's getting," said the boy with the camera.

"That's all Green's ever got," said the boy behind the stick.

Green laughed. "No, man, y'know f'real that was just *nice*," he said again, smiling down at the girl. Hers was the only living body they'd photographed that week.

*

Tetsuo is in his white suit, near the shade of the pomegranate trees, at the far end of the border fence. He has waited for her before opening the hive. She walks to him across the yellow grass, still wearing her bathing suit beneath the white protective gear and mesh mask. She sweats. There is no breeze. His back is turned to her and he is motionless. He is waiting with great restraint, and will not begin until she is standing beside him.

She checks once more for gaps at her ankles and neck, makes sure she is sealed in, runs her gloved hands over the mesh in front of her face, looking for holes.

Today they will check the bees for mites. They will see if they are sick, if some of them have brought mites home to the hive and exposed the queen. They will probably administer medicine to them. They will scoop clumps of their delicate bodies off of the combs and examine the cells. They will see who is being fed what by whom, and who is ready to break through their cell and be born into the binary life. Who is ready to learn the mapping flights, and who has died and been reabsorbed. She and Tetsuo will be together inside the circumambient hum. The hum that has dimension. Today they will just examine things, she and Tetsuo. The girl and Tetsuo.

She knows not to be distracted now at work because she doesn't like to get stung. But while she stands beside him she thinks of their names, hers and Tetsuo's, again and again, and to her growing anxiety, sees herself taking satisfaction in the names being mentioned together in conversation, or being printed together at the bottom of apiary paperwork, or even better, side by side as signatures on invoices for supplies.

Most of the time they are together they cannot even see one another's eyes, cannot see one another's form. And their voices are muffled through the masks, sound different because of the heat and an increased difficulty breathing.

Tetsuo Uber is the great-great-grand son of the inventor of the hanging frame. The file cabinet-like constructions that serve as a template for the bees' production. The white boxes that can be seen, in other places, stacked in lone meadows, or by the crests of highways, somewhere near fall flowers, near berry bushes, near orchards. The white boxes that are seen inside of this place, at the corners of concrete and wire.

Tetsuo can do this work in his sleep. Slowly and meticulously he carries it out with a preoccupied and resigned grace. Together now they can do this work without talking, without saying a word until they are sitting on the benches in the packaging plant. Sitting between the changing rooms with their masks off and with twelve or so bees flying in random arcs about the room.

Their faces are always streaked with sweat at this time and they smoke and shuffle over periodically in their baggy gear to drink from the water fountain. And again she pictures their names together, typed or as signatures, spoken, or on paper crumpled together.

Tetsuo is ten years older than she. Pale in the heat like no one she's ever seen. Arms dotted with the raised scabs of stings. She has taken this apprenticeship in the apiary because there is nothing else to do and nowhere else to go, besides the swimming pool, and the grass surrounding the swimming pool, and the dust road that sides up nicely to the perimeter fence. She took this apprenticeship because she gets to work in the field instead of the factory. And these details factor into the dysteleology that she considers somehow to be 'decisions' she has made—a kind of self determination brought about by fate; brought about by narrowing the concentric circles of provenience.

The girl has, as far as she is concerned, actively looked for unpaid agricultural work in what may, or, depending on your lexicon and affiliation, may not be 'zones of disaccord'; places that may no longer matter, or may soon become unmapped. And she has determined that this work will be instructive down to the cellular level. That this work will rebuild (through the resistance to stings and the consumption of honey) whatever depredation it is that now floats the helicopter day trips of armed demigods with telephoto lenses. That keeps them weaving a rope of sand, keeps them hovering between corpses and the exposed breasts of women in work camps.

Tetsuo had no such metaphysical ideology. He had abandoned it when the girl showed up, taken her work for his, and then taken on the task of pulling it apart through various silences, indolent preoccupations and calculated inattention, thereby exposing her to a process that had long been keeping him sane. He taught her only because he recognized the seed of obsessiveness already in her. And her devotion to faithlessness. Or maybe it was a devotion to fate.

In the absence of progress he could turn to his name or he could turn to his easy talents, the million things he did well, that passed the time, that brought him outside of all the reasons he was there. A reality constructed around the self, just as the girl's was constructed around chaos. In the absence of progress he could accept that absences were common, were the architecture of his current life.

Sometime around last year it became evident that she wouldn't be leaving. That her term at the camp was indefinite and it was then that he asked her if she knew anything about entomology. She took this question to be a couched metaphor for knowledge of secret worlds, and joked about it. Believing in secret worlds himself he took her on, to show her by example every single day that they existed, and to verbally refute, in every way, their existence.

Now in the packaging plant she hands him the shipping forms for a case of propolis and he signs his name beside hers. But her name never appears just as it is. Her name has numbers that follow: detainee number and housing code number. The new apiary paperwork has places for signatures and also has her numbers printed directly on the forms. There are boxes of forms with these numbers printed just beside two blank spaces. These numbers are also printed on the inside of her boots and on the back inside collar of her protective suit. Neither of them have ever mentioned these numbers, not even when the year's shipment of new invoices arrived with the codes already on them, nor when she showed up in the changing room to find her clothes marked with the stenciled numbers. They said nothing about it. It was a permanence that could mark some kind of bitter affiance, but marked instead more of nothing, more of the details that could only mean nothing.

He handed her back the invoice and they separated, after one more drink of water, to sleep.

*

That night she dreams that she is lying beside him in his bed. She has never seen his bed nor pictured it, yet here it is in the dream, covered in orange and dark-gray sheets. She is lying beside him in her protective gear with one glove missing, with one hand exposed. She writes on his body with the tip of her index finger. His skin is smooth like paper and he doesn't move. He is aware but doesn't move, just feels her and goes on breathing normally and there is no response—just her knowledge that he feels it and is awake. She spells his name on his stomach and then her invisible name over it. She writes about coming to that place. About its proximity to places she was before, about the difference in time zones, about the measurements of exoskeletons and the administered dosage of ergot and milk of bismuth. She writes about the algae, growing thick as moss on the inner walls of the swimming pool. And about the pieces of the waxy comb she chews to keep from being hungry.

His mind decodes the motion of her skin on his. He reads what she's spelling, reads the story as he lies beneath the orange and gray sheets in the dark room now abandoned of heat. A single lethargic bee crawls near the corner of the windowsill and she notices that it makes no sound. That Tetsuo's breathing makes no sound, that her story makes no sound. And again in the silent dream she writes their invisible names. And his sheets are slowly drained of color by the morning sun, which burns the room to white like the flash of a photograph taken from a helicopter, or the flash of a mortar as it hits a building, and in the blindness of the flash you do not think about what, if anything, was inside. Its disappearance is enough, light itself as if heralding a new beginning in absences, has absorbed the structure. And it is like this in the silent dream as well, even the dark corners and the bedframe slide rapidly into overexposure, become white light. And still asleep she hears the sirens that signal the start of the workday and the room she's never seen disappears.

*

Breakfast is something she is now allowed to eat in her room. After years the regimen has become more monastic than military. She picks up a pound of margarine, a pound of rice, two loaves of white bread, coffee, four apples, a vacuum-packed bag of dried beef, and two packs of Philip Morris cigarettes every week at the billets. It's usually more than enough for two or three meals. She takes honey as a vitamin. The short timers and the people who've just arrived eat in the kitchen. They don't pretend that they are anywhere else—like home—like an apartment or a hotel or a college internship, or even more pathetically, at an apprenticeship to some kind of artisan, some kind of genetically or ancestrally superior scientist. They do not go to the pool, even though they can. No one goes to the pool but the girl. They are housed one or two or five to a barracks. Most of their work is in the factories, and some of them are employed, what can be called employed, in the medical-testing facilities.

Tetsuo Uber is serving his sentence too, from inside a green, shingled house on a slight rise to the east of the apiary, but still inside the fence. He has a bicycle, and a ring of keys, a cat, an account at a bank, and a garden of grasses and stones. When the helicopters cease to pass, Tetsuo will not be traded for another living body, nor for a dead body, nor pieces of a dead body, nor for information. When the helicopters cease to pass no one will show up to debrief him. He will put on his yellow helmet, put his cat in a side pouch, and ride his bicycle away.

Or when the helicopters cease to pass nothing will happen. No one will be traded, or debriefed. No one will go home and there will be silence, there will be winter. The girl and Tetsuo will produce honey for no one to pick up. The women in the medical facility and the women in the factory will wander away, and their procurators will shrug. The difference between authority and the lack of it having had, after all, no real distinction. Several years investment in the outskirts of inhumanity will have been dissolved by the day to day, by common language, by the unspeakable, undeniable likenesses in form, and all that form disguises. People—even the girl—can remember that California wasn't always like this. Or maybe she thinks, they can remember that it was always something like this.

In any case, she knows that believing these things is a luxury she has because of Tetsuo. She does not work in the med-test. Her skin is not a petri dish for variations on entropy, nor is it the pale thin landscape for chemical burns, observed with a lovers steady mastery of the detail, because of Tetsuo. She is not looking into human eyes that look into her human eyes, while feeding her things that do not yet have names. Nor is she sitting with her mind in blank repose as she helps build some or other mysterious item for deployment.

She keeps bees. Tetsuo has always kept bees. She swims between the tile crosses at the ends of algae-covered lap lanes, and this is not the apocalypse of her dreams. This is no uncovering. No peeling back the surface to reveal anew, Adam and Eve amongst the rubble, back to back a four-legged creature that can at last think and do on its own, and for itself, without the scams of history. Without the practical jokes of ballistics. She knows that nothing has yet converged. Nothing has yet become epiphanic here and now inside the gate. But this doesn't mean that it won't. Every time the girl lifts the lid of the white box, every time she slides the frames up, exposing the ordered hexagons to the light, she feels her dreamed uncovering being made manifest. She feels Blake's Emanation has at last been made able-bodied, has been grafted forever to the languid form of man. She knows that it exists because knowing is all you have with something like that. Faith. Knowing that it is Emanation, unseen, but captured in the space between fingertip and fingertip just before its descent into that uninspired meat that is itself so perfect in form.

She thinks about these things not just because of the reproductions of the Capella de Sistina that she has seen, but also because she has seen Tetsuo's veined white hands as he suits up, and later as he lights his cigarette. Because she has seen that same languidness in him, a defeat or inertia, or simply a biding, waiting.

Even so, what is referred to as "the current situation" is not the apocalypse of her dreams. And Emanation has infused no form with brilliance and gravity here, no matter the reading she did in the public library, or the reproductions of reproductions her mind provides her with, no matter the world of division. The world of bees, the world of nonexistent numbers like zero or one. Like her signature or Tetsuo's.

*

Every day is not the same, though it follows its routines. Every day she gets more information. In her room she has books—packets really—with information printed on one side of the page. On the blank side she draws schematics with the stub of a grease pencil, draws new homes for the *Apis Meliflora* and draws their imagined flight patterns. The packets are dog eared and worn and appear to be readings for part of an entomology course. The pencil is nearly worn away to nothing. She shows these drawings to Tetsuo one day before opening the hive and he squints at them through the mask. This breaks the silence of their normal routine.

"I see," he says with great inflection, and actually laughs. She sees the mask move slightly as he nods. "Why do you think they'll produce more under this construction?"

"It expands the space for brood cells without having to stack another super."

"Well, then your measurements are wrong," he says, and from the sound of his voice, she can tell he's smiling, though she can't see his face.

"The numbers are a guess," she tells him. "I don't want to make it heavier. I just want to compress things."

"You're not taking into account the decrease in size of worker pharyngeal glands over time. Under this schematic more milk has to be produced for the larva, at the same time that the glands in brood workers are shrinking to prepare them for foraging flight."

"I considered it," she says. "It would require an initial purchase of more workers, but this will be compensated for after the new brood matures."

"Or it would require more fertilization, to produce more females. You've not simplified anything. You can assume the hive will self-regulate, especially species *Meliflora*, but you can't predict the initial response. The Uber design has remained unchanged for over one hundred and twenty years."

"Which means very little," the girl says. "They'll use whatever template you give them."

"No," he says. "Sometimes they leave. All of them. Even *Meli-flora*."

He tossed her drawing lightly to the ground and pumped the tiny hand held bellows. The smell of burning newspaper and grass filled the air. She lifted the lid of the white box and he watched as she slid the frame out and examined the bees while they moved *en masse* toward their food. Their conversations always took on the quality of thinking aloud, of talking to oneself. Placing sounds, words in a landscape of nothing, and then maneuvering around them. Like the *Meliflora*, she thinks, whose home is made almost entirely out of their own physiology, and the processing of particles of yellow dust, a saffron veil, that hardly catches the light.

"They think the world outside is on fire," the girl says, watching them crawl through the smoke, "and there they go to fortify themselves for flight."

*

Every day is not the same, even for the bees. Even though the world burns down, and then ceases to burn down with great regularity. Through ruse they are sufficiently distracted so that they might be observed. So that Tetsuo and the girl might gaze down into that ancestral hall without antipathy. So that they might squint through the mesh and smoke at an unbeholdable world.

*

The longer she is there, the more her thoughts seem to well from no clear source. Sitting in her room after swimming, she goes over the schematic again. But it becomes something to rest her eyes on, as she thinks and eats rice with her hands.

She remembers a story she read just before the welfare-to-work program merged with the state's correctional institutions, about a week before the global work opportunities act was passed, and people were moved to encampments where there was work for the defense effort or work for the drug and fuel effort. And where x's and y's that stood for unfathomable tricks of the body's design determined where you'd be sent. She spent most of her days in the public library back then, as she still had a valid library entrance card, and it was there she read about the fisherman and his soul. And this, she thinks, is truly the story of man. This, she thinks, is the apocalypse of the time, of the "current situation." No beautiful uncovering, no four-legged creature returned to itself, spine to spine, its head a world of sight, of perception, back to back for complete protection. The uncovering of the fisherman is instead a dissection of a kind. He stands by the sea and cuts his soul away from himself at the feet, using a special knife. And he goes to live in the ocean with the nereid he is in love with, and no one knows what it is she does or says. Every year his soul comes to the shore and begs for him to return. Bribes him with the riches of intellect and experience it has gained by wandering. And every year the fisherman refuses, and stays submerged with his love in the uterine sea. After several years the soul becomes deranged and comes back pleading telling stories of his thefts and mockeries and finally murders. The fisherman recoils completely in disgust at what his soul has done, and he goes deeper into the ocean with his undine, while his soul weeps in caves carved out by the sea. How could it do anything else but beg and plead and kill without its heart? This is the apocalypse of man, she thinks. All soul. Opportunistic soul, starving soul. Gorged on blood until there is no more, and weeping to its own form for reconciliation. Pleading for the return of the thing that will make it do right.

What is the state of the pacific? she wonders. Last time she saw it, it was nighttime and the black ocean lapped at the coast. How is it to swim there? When she swims in the pool she sees the square crosses in tile and she swims to them expecting the green that creeps into the cracks and over their surface to be soft, to have dimension like a cushion of moss. She reaches out to it but jerks her hand away at the feel of its slickness. Where do these compulsions and reflexes come from? They are like a mirror in their opposing sameness.

Before her apprenticeship she had never been stung by a bee. The first week she went to work she was stung often. It always caught her by surprise. The hum had a lulling effect and she was usually concentrating on lifting one of the frames, and she would shout, surprising herself, the same way it always surprised her when her hand jerked back and settled itself against her chest at the feel of the algae, when even her knees drew themselves up. One time when she was stung just inside her ear, she shouted loudly and tears streamed out of her eyes all at once from nowhere. Tetsuo set down the smoldering canister and pulled off his mesh mask and he grabbed her by the shoulders. "When that happens," he said angrily, bees landing on his skin, beginning to crawl into the neck of the white suit, "You stay. Inside. Your body." And he shook her firmly to punctuate each word. The hum raised in pitch and he slid the frame back into the super, and stood still to avoid being stung himself. She nodded inside the mask and hood, the tiny dart still in her ear—a spike with an abdomen loosely connected to it. A single eviscerated bee lay dying in the well of her collarbone.

And she could see then that Tetsuo would understand about the fisherman. And all she wanted right then was more of what she'd read; the rising world of waters dark and deep. Or to read it to him. No heat, no hum, no baking dust, no songs of artillery. She whispered the words bathyorographical, thalassographical, terriginous, in her mind, to stop her eyes from running.

Seven helicopters passed over the pool in the afternoon. They were not on voyeur maneuvers. They were not passing low enough to cause a breeze, nor moving slowly enough to see her swim.

Whatever break, whatever slowdown in the month's worth of action just over the fence and around the second visible hill is done—columns of black rise in the distance accompanied by the smell of burning rubber, and again the continuous sounds of deployment resonate through the dry landscape. The sounds of reverberating beaten air, anticipated and shrugged off —and the faces of the flack-jacketed Adoni invoke no more compassion than the arrival of a box of dormant drones.

These past four years would have been college. She remembers absently. She would have been in college had she not been living in a room at the YWCA when various state and federal bureaucratic mergers of the "current situation" had taken place. If the night guard hadn't repeatedly found her sleeping in the stacks of the public library, and if the word "vagrant" hadn't appeared on certain copies of forms with her name typed on them, she might have been put in college. There were other women there who would have been in college too. Some of them had even finished school, or been working for years already.

Vagrant is the filthiest word she can think of and she can't make it stick to her regardless of the Y or the public library or other places she'd sat in for too long. Vagrant is what the fisherman's soul was. Vagrant: written on the form you sign to get yourself a free trip to California. Enough helicopters passing over the work camp and one of them is bound to drop down long enough to pick up a clever vagrant and set her down again somewhere outside the fence. A vagrant can sign her name in the sand with a stick and not need anyone else's signature beside it. A vagrant can walk from there. Or could have, if it wasn't so dry, if it weren't for the mines. If it weren't for having the only good job there. If it weren't for Tetsuo's closely shorn hair or the way he hardly ever needed to shave, but when there was stubble on his face it was fine and blond-gray. If it weren't for the way he held his hands in repose or the way he held them when he was working on something delicate, like administering drugs to insects, how his middle finger was raised slightly above the rest. It is not the pale skin at his wrist, she thinks. A vagrant isn't held back by the blue veins beneath the pale skin at someone's wrist.

She mentions the helicopters as they sit across from one another on the benches in the packaging plant. And as she does, she pictures their blades spelling her name and then his in the gray sky. She hears the whump of their blades beat out the syllables of their names. She sees the strange arcs of bees flying in loose curved letters.

Tetsuo lights his cigarette and leans down to unzip the suit where it connects to his boot. There is in him an infuriating acceptance that the girl thinks borders on boredom. When she talks to him, she is conscious of sounding naive. She knows that they are outside the culture of the work camp. Connected only by forms and shipments, stops at the billets to pick up food, and low snippets of overheard conversation. She knows that her zeal for working with the bees is shared by him even though it's routine. She has seen him every day for two years, and in most of that time he has worn the white suit. In all of that time they have spoken of bees and the current situation until the two topics merge. Until parasite-infested bees and da Vinci's beautiful machines, piloted by boys with guns, are the same. Until the hive they destroy the same, their light jerky movements the same. Until the love of the one and the hatred of the other is the same. The beautiful vehicle with the poetry of its design, and the hated parasite.

He pulls off his boots now and places his bare feet on the tile.

"I'll come with you to the pool," he says. It's awkward in his mouth.

She nods as she walks over to drink from the fountain.

"Tomorrow," he says. "After we look at the *Apis Meliflora*."

*

That night she dreams of the fisherman, dreams she is with him in a cathedral of sound in the black Pacific. The water itself is made of voices—a choir whose symphonics shift in weight and density, a varied and seamless noise. The fisherman's happiness has its own treble, and the Loreli too, with her green scales, has a voice of unbearable beauty. All of these sounds converge and contain within them the thick, sated, sleepy voices of the hive. The sound permeates everywhere, presses against her eyes and soaks into her pores, into her internal organs. The fisherman's home is bare, and the ocean is full of things that cannot be seen. And he shows her his empty home with such pride. So deep within the ocean it's invisible. He gestures for her to look around, and she sees now that his teeth are made of shells— his tongue a weed that sticks out slightly between them—pressing on their shiny concave interiors to suppress a joyous laugh. He is down there in his happiness all body and heart. "But the sound that flows through them," she asks, "whose song is it?" He swims with his wife and her shoulders are white. He shakes his head at the girl, shrugs. And she realizes that the song is his soul's. The cathedral of sound is the soul's pleading, amplified as it sinks to the body. Whose cries could be so beautiful as they echo there? His soul's misery from across the shore descends, distorted to become his hearts delight. To become the entertainment of his love. To become the music they live by, their only home, a landscape of its own, beneath the sky's dark mirror, inside the sea's heavy belly. Their only and endless song.

*

The girl is waiting for Tetsuo in the heat by the concrete edge of the inground pool. She is facing him, cross-legged on the cement. She has never seen his legs, his collar bone, his bare shoulders, and now he walks wearing only gray shorts and thick black rubber sandals. He is dressed to swim—bare chested with a pair of goggles pushed up on his forehead, and holding another facemask in his hands. His shoulders are straight and she sees the symmetry of his movements as he approaches. She can see the raised welts of stings on his pale legs and chest. She is watching him approach, she realizes, with great restraint.

High above them the spinning black crosses of helicopter blades pass in loose formation. Their sound is muffled by their distance from the ground and the direction of the wind. There are many of them, a cloud of them. *What's that called?* She wonders, *a swarm? a flock? like with crows—is it called a murder? A murder of helicopters passing?*

Her suit is black and her skin is not white like Tetsuos, but tanned, burnt, peeling between the shoulder blades. Her hair is not red and blond-gray like his but black like the helicopters, dull-metallic looking because of the sun and chlorine and dust. A gun metal, washed-out black.

She continues to watch his approach and feels she is looking at him naked. She fights the embarrassment welling in her about not seeing him in his protective suit.

"We received a box of *Apis Dorsata*," he tells her by way of greeting. He hands her the diving mask he's been carrying, and squats before her on the concrete, feet flat, arms extended, elbows resting on his knees.

"We'll have to put them directly between the trees," she says, strapping the mask to her forehead. The rubber is worn and loose and the edges of the straps are hard and crumbly.

"Exactly," he nods at her. "Or else they'll abscond."

"No one raises *Dorsata*," she says.

"We do now."

"The *Dorsata* is the ancestor of our swarm. We can put them by the pomegranate tree and hope they'll be happy enough to stay. But they're still hard." She shakes her head. "They're too big for one thing. And they have those stings, those…" As she says it she understands why they've been sent the *Dorsata*. She remembers reading about the Egyptians feeding bees poisonous flower nectar and then using the honey they produced to kill. Nothing changes in three thousand years, she thinks and raises her eyebrows at him unconsciously. The *Dorsata* are lethal on their own. "People are interested in them because of their stings."

"But that's not why we're interested in them."

"That's why they were shipped here," she says matter of factly.

He nods. "But that has no bearing on our own interest." His simplification is something beyond denial. And she is forced to nod too. It's the collective details that form the autonomy in every slavery. The slavery in every individual decision. The compulsion and the reflex, the opposing symmetries. Eighty thousand bees in the hive hear, with the hairs on their legs, a song that tells them where the food is and each bee sings its own song of proximity with its body, each message just slightly different. The *Dorsata* have their separate stings, and their lack of loyalty to Uber's hanging frame. And every woman over at the med-test facility walks there on her own. Because they have all, she understands now, looking at Tetsuo's scarred and solid nakedness, left the body. Like the fisherman's soul. Like the miserable murdering soul, they have left.

All but the *Dorsata*. All but Tetsuo, and because of Tetsuo's admonitions, the girl. They have left the body like the bee left its soft stomach and spike in her ear. Every one of them there is languishing like that *Meliflora* had, unnoticed, dying, dismembered. Their last involuntary violence having pulled them inside out.

He sits down next to her, slips off his sandals and puts his feet in the water. Then he slides in and stands, strapping the goggles over his eyes. She pulls the mask down over her face and steps off the side to stand beside him. It is only now that someone else is with her, that she notices how green the water is.

They step and glide apart from one another and without saying more begin to swim, in their separate lanes, to the separate black crosses on the other side. Everything is clear with the mask on—the opposite of the mesh mask—and she sees now that the water is full of strange particulate life. She sees sunlight cutting through the water to illuminate the gray cement floor that slants beneath the horizontal shadow of her body. It turns the algae-covered walls bright, even white in patches. She's seen light like this in landscape paintings of the American Midwest—cutting through the clouds. Somehow the effect is more beautiful, more permanent, shining through water. She sees shadows of helicopters passing, eclipsing her vision, turning the floor of the pool dark, erasing the black crosses, then disappearing again so that things might shine gray and green once more.

After a few of these laps in light and shadow she sees that Tetsuo is standing in the shallow end. He is done swimming, and she crosses back, reemerging to stand beside him.

"It was refreshing," he says. Then, "keep the mask," and he pulls himself up and walks away barefoot, sandals dangling by their back straps from the ring and index fingers of his left hand.

The girl says nothing, but moves into his lane by the wall and begins to swim again. Through the mask it is clear that something has changed. As she nears the cross, the algae seems to have thinned out. She treads water close to the edge, peering at the walls, at shapes smoothed into the growth, revealing the tile and cement beneath.

He has written her name in the slick green life. At the center of the cross, with his fingertip he has written her name. Followed by no numbers, followed by no other name. And she reads it inside that green and luminous rectangle, underground and underwater, while above, the noiseless swarm of spinning blades cuts the light in two.

THE WEDDING

Had it not been for the cameras, had it not been for the technology, you wouldn't have seen it at all and we would have had to just tell you about it, my bridesmaids and I.

We would have had to say the day was quiet and that it was raining so lightly it was easy to forget that it was raining. Little beads of moisture built up on your skin and clothes but didn't break, didn't penetrate, didn't get you wet, until realizing they were there, you passed your hand over them.

The buildings were white all around us, and despite the misty atmosphere, the sky was a tremendous cloudless blue radiating above the city.

We stopped at a candy store on the way to the gates.

Since I had no sisters, my bridesmaids came in with me, and we sat at the empty counter together.

Because it was my wedding day, they were dressed in black. Because it was my wedding day, I was naked. Their heads were covered. My hair was jeweled with mist. We commented on how traditional we must look, and on how lucky we were that the weather turned out as it had.

As we sat together, my bridesmaids removed their hoods to reveal their short, straight black hair, and the tallest bridesmaid ordered milkshakes for us.

This is clear on the surveillance film. She smiles brightly and puts her book to the side, and then she asks for the milkshakes.

In the film you can see the tile of the counter and the glass, filled with rotating trays of salted nuts, behind us. Later surveillance footage would capture us at the bookstore looking for copies of Paolo Freire's *Pedagogy of the Oppressed*, but in this particular film we sat before the revolving almonds and cashews, drinking cold sweet drinks, with what looked like a layer of condensation covering our clothes and skin.

Later footage would reveal that we had somehow obtained flowers. This would have had to have happened between three thirty and five p.m. Wherever we got the flowers there was no camera. We got them down by the railroad tracks. They were purple and white phlox and they were very fragrant. They were very sweet. My bridesmaids held bunches of them in their pale hands and walked beside me up the road.

This is captured around five thirty-five by a camera mounted on a streetlamp.

My bridesmaids were concerned that I have all the traditional things: the Freire book, the railroad phlox, the ice cream at the candy store counter. Because without these things they felt my marriage would be doomed, and the enormous dowry they paid the collection agency my groom was registered with would be for naught.

So it was with our phlox, book, traditional dress and nudity, we went together to the stone archway of our misty town to dig.

This was captured by several different cameras, as the stone archway has many cameras mounted on it.

We set the flowers down in a circle near the site. My bridesmaids paid the shovel rental fee at the ticket booth, which stood just next to the remains of the rollercoaster. The rollercoaster, now long abandoned, its little two-man cars crashed and rusty just beside the archway. The shovel renter gave them two shovels, and we nervously and happily took turns stabbing the ground beside the ring of phlox, to unearth my groom.

We did not sweat, though the sky was bright and the temperature, even towards evening, was warm. The mist kept us cool. We dug at a steady pace and talked about the Freire book. If we did not unearth my groom by seven p.m., we would have to pay an extra four dollars to the shovel rental. The digging was not hard; the ground was soft in the place where he had chosen.

At six fifteen my bridesmaids began to dig more gently—to scrape the dirt away instead of jabbing the ground with the points of their shovels. At six nineteen they uncovered my groom's shoulder. After that it was easy to guess where the rest of his form was buried, and to dig him out. His skin was dirty and his hair was thick with mud. When he raised his head and opened his eyes, my bridesmaids moved in closer. For I had told them about the jagged gold ring that surrounded his pupil, and the flecks of black in the pale iris that appeared in only one of his eyes, like the remains of something shattered.

Once uncovered he stood up in the hole, caked with mud. Two of my bridesmaids stood at his sides. They took his hands as he stepped from the hole and walked with him into the ring of railroad phlox where I stood watching his naked muscled form. Where I stood waiting to take him from my bridesmaids.

We smiled then. We laughed. My bridesmaids returned the shovels to the ticket booth. The mist upon our skin at last began to feel slick and wet. And we kissed the betrothal kiss with breath of milk and sugar, with breath of clay and rain. Our hands curved over the shoulders of the other. Our chests a hair's width apart.

My bridesmaids at the ticket booth take down their hoods and smile, laugh, chat with the shovel renter.

This is captured by the archway-mounted cameras. This betrothal kiss among the flowers. And also our walk through the town gates, out towards the remains of the rollercoaster, our heads slipping below the frame as we duck beneath the rusted tracks. And then we are gone.